THE EARL'S
CONVENIENT
WIFE

THE EARL'S CONVENIENT WIFE

BY

MARION LENNOX

First published in Great Britain 2015
by Mills & Boon, an imprint of Harlequin (UK) Limited,
Large Print edition 2015
Eton House, 18-24 Paradise Road,
Richmond, Surrey, TW9 1SR

© 2015 Marion Lennox

ISBN: 978-0-263-25701-4

Harlequin (UK) Limited's policy is to use papers that
are natural, renewable and recyclable products and made
from wood grown in sustainable forests. The logging
and manufacturing processes conform to the legal
environmental regulations of the country of origin.

Printed and bound in Great Britain
by CPI Antony Rowe, Chippenham, Wiltshire

With thanks to Rose M,
my new and wonderful neighbour and friend.
Gardening will never be the same again.

CHAPTER ONE

MARRY...

There was deathly silence in the magnificent library of the ancient castle of Duncairn. In specially built niches round the walls were the bottles of whisky Jeanie had scraped to afford. Weirdly, that was what she was focusing on. What a waste. How much whisky could she fit in a suitcase?

How many scores of fruitcakes would they make? There was no way she was leaving them behind. For him. For her prospective bridegroom?

What a joke.

She'd been clinging to the hope that she might keep her job. She knew the Lord of Duncairn didn't like her, but she'd worked hard to give Duncairn Castle the reputation for hospitality it now enjoyed.

It didn't matter. Her efforts were for nothing. This crazy will meant she was out on her ear.

'This must be a joke.' Alasdair McBride, the sixteenth Earl of Duncairn, sounded appalled. It was no wonder. She stood to lose her job. Alasdair stood to lose his...fiefdom?

'A last will and testament is never a joke.' Edward McCraig, of the prestigious law firm McCraig, McCraig & McFerry, had made the long journey from Edinburgh to be at today's funeral for Eileen McBride—Alasdair's grandmother and Jeanie's employer. He'd sat behind Jeanie in the Duncairn Kirk and listened to the eulogies with an air of supressed impatience. He wished to catch the last ferry back to the mainland. He was now seated in one of the library's opulent chairs, reading the old lady's wishes to her only surviving grandson—and to the live-in help.

He shuffled his papers and pushed his glasses further down his nose, looking at neither of them. Crazy or not, Eileen's will clearly made him uncomfortable.

Jeanie looked at Alasdair and then looked away. This might be a mess, but it had little to do with her, she decided. She went back to counting whisky bottles. Maybe three suitcases? She only had one, but there were crates in the castle cellars. If she was brave enough to face the dark and the spiders...

Could you sell whisky online?

She glanced back at Alasdair and found his gaze was following hers, along the line of whisky. With an oath—a mixture of fury and shock—he took three glasses from the sideboard and poured. Soda-sized whiskies.

The lawyer shook his head but Jeanie took hers with gratitude. The will had been a nasty shock. It was excellent whisky and she couldn't take it all with her.

But it did need to be treated with respect. As the whisky hit home she choked and sank onto one of the magnificent down-filled sofas. A cloud of dog hair rose around her. She really had to do something about Eileen's dogs.

Or not. This will said they were no longer her problem. She'd have to leave the island. She couldn't take the dogs and she loved them. This castle might be over-the-top opulent, but she loved it, too. She felt...befuddled.

'So how do we get around this?' Clearly the whisky wasn't having the same effect on Alasdair that it was on her. His glass was almost empty. She looked at him in awe. Actually she'd been looking sideways at Alasdair all afternoon. Well, why not? He might be arrogant, he might have despised her from the first time he'd met her, but he'd always been worth looking at.

Alasdair McBride was thirty-seven years old, and he was what Jeanie's granny would have described as a man to be reckoned with. Although he didn't use it, his hereditary title fitted him magnificently, especially today. In honour of his grandmother's funeral he was wearing full highland regalia, and he looked awesome.

Jeanie always had had a weakness for a man in a kilt, and the Duncairn tartan was gorgeous. Okay, the Earl of Duncairn was gorgeous, she conceded. Six foot two in his stockinged feet, with jet-black hair and the striking bone structure and strength of the warrior race he'd so clearly descended from, Alasdair McBride was a man to make every eye in the room turn to him. The fact that he controlled the massive Duncairn financial empire only added to his aura of power, but he needed no such addition to look what he was—a man in control of his world.

Except…now he wasn't. His grandmother's will had just pulled the rug from under his feet.

And hers. *Marry?* So much for her quiet life as the Duncairn housekeeper.

'You can't get around it,' the lawyer was saying. 'The will is inviolate.'

'Do you think…?' She was testing her voice for the first time since the bombshell had landed. 'Do you think that Eileen might possibly have been…have been…?'

'Lady McBride was in full possession of her senses.' The lawyer cast her a cautious look as if he was expecting her to disintegrate into hysterics. 'My client understood her will was slightly… unusual…so she took steps to see that it couldn't be overturned. She arranged a certificate of medical competency, dated the same day she made the will.'

Alasdair drained the rest of his whisky and poured another, then spun to look out of the great bay window looking over the sea.

It was a magnificent window. A few highland cattle grazed peacefully in the late-summer sun, just beyond the ha-ha. Further on, past rock-strewn burns and craggy hills, were the remnants of a vast medieval fortress on the shoreline. Two eagles were soaring effortlessly in the thermals. If he used binoculars, he might even see otters in the burns running into the sea, Jeanie thought. Or deer. Or…

Or her mind was wandering. She put her glass down, glanced at Alasdair's broad back and felt a twist of real sympathy. Eileen had been good to her already, and in death she owed her nothing. Alasdair's loss, however, was appalling. She might not like the man, but he hadn't deserved this.

Oh, Eileen, what were you thinking? she demanded wordlessly of her deceased employer—but there was nothing Jeanie could do.

'I guess that's it, then,' she managed, addressing herself to the lawyer. 'How long do I have before you want me out?'

'There's no rush,' the lawyer told her. 'It'll take a while to get the place ready for sale.'

'Do you want me to keep trading? I have guests booked until the end of next month.'

'That would be excellent. We may arrange for you to stay even longer. It'd be best if we could sell it as a going concern.'

'No!' The explosion was so fierce it almost rocked the room. Alasdair turned from the window and slammed his glass onto the coffee table so hard it shattered. He didn't seem to notice.

'It can't happen.' Alasdair's voice lowered, no longer explosive but cold and hard and sure.

'My family's entire history, sold to fund…dogs' homes?'

'It's a worthy cause,' the lawyer ventured but Alasdair wasn't listening.

'This castle is the least of it,' he snapped. 'Duncairn is one of the largest financial empires in Europe. Do you know how much our organisation gives to charity each year? Sold, it could give every lost dog in Europe a personal attendant and gold-plated dog bowl for the rest of its life, but then it's gone. Maintained, we can do good—we *are* doing good. This will is crazy. I'll channel every penny of profit into dog care for the next ten years if I must, but to give it away…'

'I understand it would mean the end of your career—' the lawyer ventured but he was cut off.

'It's not the end of my career.'

If Lord Alasdair had had another glass, Jeanie was sure it'd have gone the way of the first.

'Do you know how many corporations would employ me? I have the qualifications and the skills to start again, but to haul apart my family inheritance on a stupid whim?'

'The thing is,' the lawyer said apologetically, 'I don't think it was a whim. Your grandmother felt your cousin treated his wife very badly and she wished to atone…'

'Here it is again. It all comes back to my wastrel cousin.' Alasdair spun around and stared at Jeanie with a look that was pretty much all contempt. 'You married him.'

'There's no need to bring Alan into this.'

'Isn't there? Eileen spent her life papering over his faults. She was blind to the fact that he was a liar and a thief, and that blind side's obviously extended to you. What was she on about? Marry Alan's widow? You? I'd rather walk on hot coals. You're the housekeeper here—nothing more. Marry anyone you like, but leave me alone.'

Her sympathy faded to nothing. 'Anyone I like?' she retorted. 'Wow. Thank you kindly, sir. As a proposal, that takes some beating.'

'It's the only proposal you're likely to get.'

'Then isn't it lucky I don't want one?'

He swore and turned again to the window. Jeanie's brief spurt of anger faded and she returned to shock.

Marriage…? To Alasdair? What *were* you thinking, Eileen? she demanded again of the departed Lady McBride.

Was she thinking the same as when she'd coerced Alan into marrying Jeanie? At least it was out in the open this time, she conceded. At least all the cards were on the table. The will spelt it out with startling clarity. It was an order to Alasdair. *Marry Jeanie, collect your inheritance, the only cost—one year of marriage. If not, inherit nothing.*

Oh, Eileen.

'I believe the time for angry words is not now.' The lawyer was clearing his papers into a neat pile, ready to depart, but his dry, lawyer's voice was sounding a warning. 'You need to be quite clear before you make rash decisions. I understand that emotions are…high…at the moment, but think about it. Neither of you are married. My Lord, if you marry Mrs McBride, then you keep almost the entire estate. Mrs McBride, if you marry His Lordship, in twelve months you get to keep the castle. That's a substantial amount to be throwing away because you can't get on.'

'The castle belongs to my family,' Alasdair snapped. 'It has nothing to do with this woman.'

'Your grandmother treated Jeanie as part of your family.'

'She's not. She's just as bad as—'

'My Lord, I'd implore you not to do—or say—

anything in haste,' the lawyer interrupted. 'Including making statements that may inflame the situation. I suggest you take a couple of days and think about it.'

A couple of days? He had to be kidding, Jeanie thought. There was only one decision to be made in the face of this craziness, and she'd made it. She looked at Alasdair's broad back, at his highland kilt, at the size of him—he was practically blocking the window. She looked at the tense set of his shoulders. She could almost taste his rage and his frustration.

Get this over with, she told herself, and she gave herself a fraction of a second to feel sorry for him again. No more, though. Protect yourself, she scolded. Get out of here fast.

'Alasdair doesn't want to marry me and why should he?' she asked the lawyer. 'And I surely don't want to marry him. Eileen was a sweetheart but she was also a conniving matriarch. She liked pulling the strings but sometimes… sometimes she couldn't see that the cost was impossibly high. I've married one of her grandsons. I'm not marrying another and that's an end to it. Thank you for coming, sir. Should I ring for the taxi to collect you, in, say, fifteen minutes?'

'That would be excellent. Thank you. You've been an excellent housekeeper to Duncairn, Mrs McBride. Eileen was very fond of you.'

'I know she was, and I loved her, too,' Jeanie said. 'But sometimes...' She glanced again at Alasdair. 'Well, the family has always been known for its arrogance. The McBrides have been ordering the lives of Duncairn islanders for generations, but this time Eileen's taken it a step too far. I guess the Duncairn ascendancy is now in freefall but there's nothing I can do about it. Good afternoon, gentlemen.'

And she walked out and closed the door behind her.

She was gone. Thankfully. Alasdair was left with the lawyer.

Silence, silence and more silence. The lawyer was giving him space, Alasdair thought, and he should be grateful.

He wasn't.

His thoughts went back to his grandfather, an astute old man whose trust in his wife had been absolute. He'd run the Duncairn financial empire with an iron fist. Deeply disappointed in his two sons—Alasdair's and Alan's respective fathers—

the old man had left control of the entire estate in the hands of Eileen.

'By the time you die I hope our sons have learned financial sense,' he'd told her. 'You can decide who is best to take over.'

But neither of his sons had shown the least interest in the estate, apart from persuading Eileen to give them more money. They'd predeceased their mother, one in a skiing accident, one from a heart attack, probably caused by spending his life in Michelin-starred restaurants.

No matter. That was history. Eileen had come from a long line of thrifty Scots, and in Alasdair she'd found a family member who shared her business acumen and more.

As they'd turned the company into the massive empire it now was, Alasdair had tried to talk his grandmother into making it a public entity, making it safe if anything had happened to either of them. She'd refused. 'I trust you,' she'd told him but she'd maintained total ownership.

And now this...

'Surely it's illegal,' he said, feeling bone weary.

'What could be illegal?'

'Coercing us into marriage.'

'There's no coercion. The way your grand-mother worded it…

'You helped her word it.'

'Mr Duncan McGrath, the firm's most senior lawyer, helped her draft it, to make sure there were no legal loopholes.' The lawyer was suddenly stern. 'She was very clear what she wanted. The will states that the entire financial empire plus any other assets she owns are to be liquidated and left in equal parts to a large number of canine charities. As an aside, she states that the only way the intentions of the will can be set aside is if you and Mrs McBride marry.'

'That woman is not a McBride.'

'She's Mrs McBride,' the lawyer repeated sternly. 'You know that she is. Your grandmother loved her and treated her as family, and your grandmother wanted to cement that relationship. The bequest to the canine charities can only be set aside if, within a month of her death, you and Mrs Jeanie McBride are legally married. To each other.'

'We both know that's crazy. Even…Mrs Mc-Bride…didn't consider it for a moment.' He ran his fingers through his hair, the feeling of exhaustion intensifying. 'It's blackmail.'

'It's not blackmail. The will is set up so that in the—admittedly unlikely—event that you marry, your grandmother provides for you as a family.'

'And if we're not?'

'Then she's done what any lonely old woman in her situation might do. She's left her fortune to dogs' homes.'

'So if we contest…'

'I've taken advice, sir. I was…astounded at the terms of the will myself, so I took the liberty to sound out a number of my colleagues. Legal advice is unanimous that the will stands.'

More silence. Alasdair reached for his whisky and discovered what he'd done. The table was covered with broken glass. He needed to call someone to clean it up.

Mrs McBride? Jeanie.

His cousin's wife had operated this place as a bed and breakfast for the past three years. As cook, housekeeper and hostess, she'd done a decent job, he'd had to concede. 'You should see how it is now,' his grandmother had told him, beaming. 'Jeanie's the best thing that's happened to this family.'

That wasn't true. Even though he conceded she'd looked after this place well, it was by her first actions he'd judged her. As Alan's wife. She'd run wild with his cousin and she'd been beside him when he'd died. Together she and Alan had broken Eileen's heart, but Eileen had never been prepared to cut her loose.

Marrying Alan had branded her, he conceded, but that brand was justified. Any fool could have seen the crazy lifestyle his cousin had been living was ruinous. The money she and Alan had thrown round... That was why she was still looking after the castle, in the hope of inheriting something more. He was sure of it. For an impoverished island lass, the McBride fortune must seem seductive, to say the least.

Seduction... By money?

If she'd married for money once before...

His mind was suddenly off on a crazy tangent that made him feel ill.

Marriage... But what was the alternative?

'So what if we *did* marry?' he demanded at last, goaded into saying it.

'Then everything reverts to how it's been,' the lawyer told him. He was watching him cautiously now, as if he half expected Alasdair to lob whisky at him. 'If you and Mrs McBride marry and stay married for a period of no less than one year, you'll legally own the Duncairn empire with all it entails, with the exception of the castle itself. Mrs McBride will own that.'

'Just this castle?'

'And the small parcel of land on the same title. Yes. They're the terms of the will.'

'Does she have a clue how much this place costs to maintain? What she gets with the bed and breakfast guests couldn't begin to touch it. And without the surrounding land...'

'I'd imagine Mrs McBride could sell,' the lawyer said, placing his papers back in his briefcase. 'Maybe to you, if you wish to continue the Duncairn lineage. But right now, that's immaterial. If you don't marry her, the castle will be part of the whole estate to be sold as one. Mrs McBride needs to consider her future with care, but maintenance of the castle is immaterial unless you marry.'

And there was the only glimmer of light in this whole impossible situation. If he didn't inherit, neither would she. It'd be great to be finally shot of her.

He didn't need this inheritance. He didn't. If he walked away from this mess, he could get a job tomorrow. There were any number of corporations that'd take his expertise.

But to walk away from Duncairn? His ancestral home...

And the company. So many people... He thought of the firm most likely to buy if he no longer had control and he felt ill. They'd merge. All his senior management... All his junior staff...Scotland was struggling after the global financial crisis anyway. How could they get new jobs?

They couldn't, and there was nothing he could do about it.

Unless...unless...

'She *has* been married before,' he said slowly, thinking aloud. He didn't like the woman one bit. He didn't trust her, but if he was careful... Initial revulsion was starting to give way to sense. 'She married my cousin so I'm assuming money's important to her. I guess—if it got me out of this mess, I might be prepared to marry. In name only,' he added hastily. 'As a business deal.'

Marriage... The idea made him feel ill. But Lords of Duncairn had married for convenience before, he reminded himself. They'd married heiresses to build the family fortunes. They'd done what had to be done to keep the estate safe.

And the lawyer was permitting himself a dry smile, as if his client was now talking like a sensible man. 'I've considered that option,' he told him. 'It would meet the requirements of the bequest—as long as you lived together.'

'Pardon?'

'Lady Eileen was very sure of what she wanted. She has…all eventualities covered.'

He exhaled and took a while to breathe again. Eventualities… 'Explain.'

'You and Mrs McBride would need to live in the same residence for a period of at least one year before the estate can be settled. However, Lady Eileen was not unreasonable. She acknowledges that in the course of your business you do need to travel, so she's made allowances. Those allowances are restrictive, however. In the twelve months from the time of your marriage there's an allowance for no more than thirty nights spent apart.'

Alasdair said nothing. He couldn't think what to say.

He'd loved his grandmother. None of what he

was thinking right now had any bearing on that love. If he had her in front of him...

'She's also taken steps to ensure that this arrangement was kept.' The lawyer coughed apologetically. 'I'm sorry, but you would need to keep to...the intent of the will.'

'You mean she'd have us watched?'

'There are funds set aside to ensure the terms are being adhered to.'

He stared at the lawyer in horror. 'You're out of your mind. Next you'll be saying you'll be checking the sheets.'

'I believe,' the lawyer said and allowed himself another wintry smile, 'that your sleeping arrangements within the one residence would be entirely up to you and your...your wife. Mind...' he allowed the smile to widen '...she's an attractive wee thing.'

'Of all the...'

'Though it's not my business to say so, sir. I'm sorry.'

'No.' Though she was, Alasdair conceded, his thoughts flying sideways again. He'd been astounded when his cousin had married her. Jeanie McBride was petite and freckled and rounded. Her soft brown shoulder-length curls, mostly tugged back into a ponytail, were nothing out of the ordinary. She didn't dress to kill. In fact, the first time he'd met her, he'd thought how extraordinary that the womanising Alan was attracted to such a woman.

But then she'd smiled at something his grandmother had said, and he'd seen what Alan had obviously seen. Her smile was like the sun coming out after rain. Her face lit and her freckles seemed almost luminescent. She had a dimple at the side of her mouth, and when she'd chuckled…

He hadn't heard that chuckle for a long time, he thought suddenly. He hadn't seen her smile, either.

In truth, he'd avoided her. His grandmother's distress over Alan's wasted life had been enough to make him avoid Jeanie and all she represented. He'd known she was caring for the castle and he acknowledged she'd seemed to be making a good job of it. She'd steered clear of him these past few months when he'd come to visit his grandmother. She'd treated him formally, as a castle guest, and he'd treated her like the housekeeper she was.

But she wasn't just a housekeeper. Right after Alan's death Eileen had said, 'She seems like a daughter to me,' and he'd thought, Uh-oh, she'll stick around until the old lady dies and hope to inherit, and now he was proved right.

She must be as shocked as he was about the will's contents. She'd get nothing unless they married…

That could be used to his advantage. His mind was racing. The only cost would be the castle.

And a year of his life…

The lawyer had risen, eager to depart. 'I'm sorry, sir. I understand I'm leaving you in a quandary but my task here was purely as messenger. I can see the taxi approaching. Mrs McBride has been efficient as always. Will you bid her farewell for me? Meanwhile, if there's anything else myself or my partners can do…'

'Tear up the will?'

'You and I both know that we can't do that. The will is watertight. From now on there's only a decision to be made, and I have no place here while you make it. Good luck, sir, and goodbye.'

CHAPTER TWO

THERE WAS TOO much to get his head around.

Alasdair paced the library, and when that wasn't big enough he took himself outdoors, through the great, grand castle entrance, across the manicured lawns, down the ha-ha and to the rough pastures beyond.

The shaggy highland cattle were still where they'd been while the lawyer had been making his pronouncements. The day had been warm and they were feeling the heat. If it got any hotter, they'd be wandering down to the sea and standing belly deep in the water, but for now they were lying on the rich summer grass, grazing where they could reach.

He loved the cattle. More, he loved this whole estate. His grandparents had made one small section of the castle liveable when his grandfather inherited, and they'd brought him here as a boy. He'd wandered the place at will, free from the demands his socialite parents put on him, free of the restrictions of being known as a rich kid. He'd fished, climbed, roamed, and when his grandmother had decided on restoration he'd been delighted.

Only that restoration had brought Jeanie into their lives.

If it hadn't been Jeanie, it would have been someone else, he thought grimly, striding down the line of battered fencing towards the bay. His grandmother's two dogs, Abbot and Costello, elegant spaniels, beautiful, fast and dumb, had loped out to join him. The smell of rabbits would be everywhere, and the dogs were going nuts trying to find them.

Alan's wife…Jeanie…

His grandmother had said she'd loved her.

He'd thought his grandmother had loved him.

'So why treat us like this?' he demanded of his departed grandmother. 'If we don't marry, we'll have nothing.'

It was blackmail. Marry… The thing was nonsense.

But the knot of shock and anger was starting to untwist. Jeanie's assessment was right—his grandmother was a conniving, Machiavellian matriarch—so he might have expected something like this. Marriage to Alan's widow... Of all the dumb...

Eileen had loved reading romance novels. He should have confiscated every one and burned them before it was too late.

He reached the bay and set himself down on a great smooth rock, a foundation stone of an ancient fortress. He gazed out to sea but his mind was racing. Option one, no inheritance. Nothing. Walk away. The thought made him feel ill.

He turned and gazed back at the castle. He'd hardly been here these past years but it had always been in his mind. In his heart?

There'd been McBrides at Duncairn Castle since almost before the dinosaurs. Would he be the one to let it go?

The woodchip industry would move in, he thought. The pastures included with the castle title were mostly wild. The castle was heritage-listed, but not the land.

There were deer watching cautiously just above the horizon, but money was in woodchips, not deer. The land would go.

Which led—sickeningly—to option two.

Marriage. To a woman he couldn't stand, but who also stood to gain by the inheritance.

He gazed around again at the cattle, at the distant deer, at the water lapping the shores, the dogs barking in the distance, the eagles…

His land. Duncairn.

Was the thing impossible?

And the more he calmed down, the more he saw it wasn't. His apartment in Edinburgh was large, with separate living quarters for a housekeeper. He'd bought the place when he and Celia were planning marriage, and afterwards he'd never seen the point of moving. He worked fourteen-, fifteen-hour days, especially now. There were things happening within the company he didn't understand. Nebulous but worrying. He needed to focus.

He still could. He could use the Edinburgh house simply to sleep. That could continue and the terms of the will would be met.

'It could work,' he reasoned. 'The apartment's big enough for us to keep out of each other's way.'

But what will she do while you're away every day? The question came from nowhere, and he briefly considered it.

'She can shop, socialise, do what other wives do.'

Wives…

He'd have a wife. After Celia's betrayal he'd sworn…

Eileen had known that he'd sworn. That was why she'd done this.

He needed to suppress his anger. What he'd learned, hard and early, was that emotion got you nowhere. Reason was everything.

'It's only for a year,' he told himself. 'There's no choice. To walk away from everything is unthinkable.'

But walking away was still an option. He had money independent of Duncairn—of course he did. When he'd first started working in the firm, his grandmother had insisted on a salary commensurate with other executives of his standing. He was well-qualified, and even without this dubious inheritance he was wealthy. He could walk away.

But Duncairn…

He turned and looked back again at the castle, a great grey mass of imposing stone built by his ancestors to last for centuries. And the company… The financial empire had drawn him in since his teens. He'd worked to make it the best in the world, and to let it go…

'I'd be able to buy the castle from her when

the year's up,' he told himself. 'You can't tell me she's not in for the main chance. If I'm the highest bidder, she'll take the money and run.'

Decision made. He rose and stretched and called the dogs.

'I'll do this,' he said out loud, addressing the ghost of his absent grandmother. 'Fine, Grandmother, you win. I'll talk to her and we'll organise a wedding. But that'll be it. It might be a wedding but it's not a marriage. If you think I'll ever be interested in Alan's leavings...'

Don't think of her like that.

But he couldn't help himself. Alan's betrayal, his gut-wrenching cruelty, was still raw after all these years and Jeanie was Alan's widow. He'd stayed away from this castle because he'd wanted nothing to do with her, but now...

'Now we'll have to share the same front door in Edinburgh,' he told himself. For a year. But a year's not so long when what's at stake is so important. *You can do it, man. Go take yourself a wife.*

She was in the kitchen. The kitchen was her solace, her joy. Cooks had been baking in this kitchen for hundreds of years. The great range took half the wall. The massive oak table, twenty feet long, was pocked and scratched from generations of chopping and rolling and kneading. The vast cobbled floor was worn from hundreds of servants, feeding thousands.

Eileen had restored the castle, making it truly sumptuous, but she'd had the sense to leave the kitchen free from modern grandeur. Jeanie had an electric oven tucked discreetly by the door. There was even a microwave and dishwasher in the vast, hall-like pantry, but the great stove was still lit as it seemed to have stayed lit forever. There was a sumptuous basket on each side for the dogs. The effect was old and warm and breathtaking.

Here was her place, Jeanie thought. She'd loved it the first time she'd seen it, and she'd found peace here.

She was having trouble finding peace now.

When in doubt, turn to scones, she told herself. After all these years she could cook them in her sleep. She didn't provide dinner for the castle guests but she baked treats for occasional snacks or for when they wandered in after dinner. She usually baked slices or a cake but right now she needed something that required no thought.

She wasn't thinking. She was *not* thinking. Marriage...

She shouldn't care. She hadn't expected to inherit anything, but to tie the estate up as Eileen had... It didn't matter how much she disliked Alasdair; this was cruel. Had Eileen really been thinking it could happen?

And even though her thoughts should be on Alasdair, on the injustice done to him, there was also a part of her that hurt. No, she hadn't expected an inheritance, but she hadn't expected this, either. That Eileen could possibly think she could organise her down that road again... Try one grandson, if that doesn't work, try another?

'What were you thinking?' she demanded of the departed Eileen.

And then she thought: Eileen hadn't been thinking. She'd been hoping.

Those last few months of her life, Eileen had stayed at the castle a lot. Her normally feisty personality had turned inward. She'd wept for Alan, but she'd also wept for Alasdair.

'His parents and then that appalling woman he almost married...they killed something in him,' she'd told Jeanie. 'If only he could find a woman like you.'

This will was a fanciful dream, Jeanie thought, kneading her scone dough. The old lady might have been in full possession of her faculties, but her last will and testament was nothing more than a dream.

'She mustn't have thought it through,' she said to herself. 'She could never have thought we'd walk away from what she saw as irresistible temptation. She'd never believe we could resist.'

But Eileen hadn't had all the facts. Jeanie thought of those facts now, of an appalling marriage and its consequences, and she felt ill. If Eileen knew what she'd done, it'd break her heart.

But what could she do about it now? Nothing. Nothing, nothing and nothing. Finally she stared down and realised what she'd been doing. Kneading scone dough? Was she out of her mind?

'There's nothing worse than tough scones,' she told the world in general. 'Except marriage.'

Two disastrous marriages… Could she risk a third?

'Maybe I will,' she told herself, searching desperately for the light side, the optimistic bit of Jeanie McBride that had never entirely been quenched. 'Eventually. Maybe I might finally find myself a life. I could go to Paris—learn to cook French pastries. Could I find myself a sexy Parisian who enjoys a single malt?'

She almost smiled at that. All that whisky had to be useful for something. If she was honest, it wasn't even her drink of choice.

But since when had she ever had a choice? There was still the overwhelming issue of her debt, she thought, and the urge to smile died. Alan's debt. The bankruptcy hung over her like a massive, impenetrable cloud. How to be optimistic in the face of that?

She glanced out of the window, at the eagles who soared over the Duncairn castle as if they owned it.

'That's what I'd really like to do,' she whispered. 'Fly. But I'm dreaming. I'm stuck.'

And then a deep masculine response from the doorway made her almost jump out of her skin.

'That's what I'm thinking.'

Her head jerked from window to doorway and he was standing there. The Lord of Duncairn.

How long had he been watching? Listening? She didn't know. She didn't care, she told herself, fighting for composure as she tossed her dough into the waste and poured more flour into her bowl. McBrides…

But this man was not Alan. She told herself that, but as she did she felt a queer jump inside.

No, he wasn't Alan. He was nothing like him. They'd been cousins but where Alan had been out for a good time, this man was rock solid. Judgemental, yes. 'Harsh' and 'condemnatory' were two adjectives that described him well—and yet, gazing at the man in the doorway, she felt the weird inside flutter that she'd felt in the library.

Attraction? She had to be joking.

He was her feudal lord, she told herself harshly. She was a peasant. And when peasantry met gentry—run!

But for now she was the cook in this man's castle. She was forced to stay and she was forced to listen.

'Jeanie, my grandmother's treated us both badly,' he said and his tone was one of conciliation. 'I don't know what you wanted but you surely can't have expected this.'

She started at that. The anger she'd heard from him had disappeared. What came through now was reason and caution, as if he wasn't sure how to proceed.

That made two of them.

'She hasn't treated me badly.' She made herself

say it lightly but she knew it was true. Eileen had had no cause to offer her a job and a livelihood in this castle. There'd been no obligation. Eileen's action had been pure generosity.

'Your grandmother has been very, very good to me,' she added, chopping butter and starting to rub it into the new lot of flour. The action was soothing—an age-old task that calmed something deep within—and almost took her mind off the sex-on-legs image standing in the doorway. Almost. 'I've loved living and working here but jobs don't last forever. I don't have any right to be here.'

'You were married to Alan. You were… You *are* family.'

It was as if he was forcing himself to say it, she thought. He was forcing himself to be nice?

'The marriage was brief and it was a disaster,' she said curtly. 'I'm no longer your family—I'm your grandmother's ex-employee. I'm happy to keep running the castle until it's sold but then… Then I'm happy to go.' Liar, liar, pants on fire, she added silently to herself. It'd break her heart to leave; it'd break her heart to see the castle sold to the highest bidder. She had so little money to go anywhere, but there was no way she was baring her heart to this man.

Right now she was almost afraid of him. He was leaning against the doorjamb, watching her. He looked a warrior, as fierce and as ruthless as the reputation of the great lineage of Duncairn chieftains preceding him.

He was no such thing, she told herself fiercely. He was just a McBride, another one, and she needed to get away from here fast.

'But if we married, you could keep the castle.'

Jeanie's hands stilled. She stood motionless. In truth, she was counting breaths, or lack of them.

He'd said it as if it were the most reasonable thing in the world. *If you give me a penny, I'll give you an apple.* It was that sort of statement.

Ten, eleven, twelve… She'd have to breathe soon.

'Maybe it's reasonable,' Alasdair continued while she wondered if her breathing intended starting again. 'Maybe it's the only sensible course of action.' He'd taken his jacket off and rolled his sleeves. His arms were folded. They were great, brawny arms, arms that gave the lie to the fact that he was a city financier. His kilt made him seem even more a warrior.

He was watching her—as a panther watched its prey?

'It'd get us both what we want,' he said, still watchful. 'Alone, we walk away from everything we've worked for. Eileen's will is a nightmare but it doesn't have to be a total disaster. We need to work around it.'

'By…marrying?' Her voice came out a squeak but she was absurdly grateful it came out at all.

'It's the only way you can keep the castle.'

'I don't want the castle.'

That stopped him. His face stilled, as if he wasn't sure where to take it from there.

'No matter what Eileen's will says, the castle should never be my inheritance,' she managed. She was fighting to keep her voice as reasonable as his. 'The castle's my job, but that's all it is. You're the Earl of Duncairn. The castle's your ancestral home. Your grandmother's suggestion might be well-meant, but it's so crazy I don't believe we should even talk about it.'

'We need to talk about it.'

'We don't. I'm sorry your grandmother has left you in such a situation but that's for you to sort. Thank you, Lord Duncairn, for considering such a mad option, but I have scones to cook. I'm mov-

42   THE EARL'S CONVENIENT WIFE

ing on. I'll work until the lawyer asks me to leave and then I'll be out of your life forever.'

Whatever he'd expected, it wasn't this. A straight-out refusal to even talk about it.

Okay, it was how he'd reacted, he decided, but he'd had an hour's walk to clear his head. This woman clearly hadn't had time to think it through.

To walk away from a castle… *This* castle.

What else was she angling for?

He watched her work for a bit while she ignored him, but if she thought he'd calmly leave, she was mistaken. This was serious.

Keep it as a business proposition, he told himself. After all, business was what he was good at. Business was what he was *all* about. Make it about money.

'I realise the upkeep would be far too much for you to keep the castle long-term,' he told her, keeping his voice low and measured. Reasoning as he talked. Maybe she was still shocked at not receiving a monetary inheritance. Maybe there was anger behind that calm façade of hers.

'The company has been funding long-term maintenance and restoration,' he continued, refusing to see the look of revulsion on her face. Revulsion? Surely he must be misreading. 'We can continue doing that,' he told her. 'If at the end of the year this inheritance goes through and you don't wish to stay, the company can buy the castle from you.'

'You could afford that?' she demanded, incredulous?

'The company's huge. It can and it seems the most sensible option. You'll find I can be more than generous. Eileen obviously wanted you looked after. Alan was my cousin. I'll do that for him.'

But at that she flashed him a look that could have split stone.

'I don't need looking after,' she snapped. 'I especially don't need looking after by the McBride men.'

He got it then. Her anger wasn't just encompassing Eileen and her will. Her anger was directed at the McBride family as a whole.

She was holding residual anger towards Alan? Why?

He and Alan had never got on and their mutual dislike had meant they never socialised. He'd met Jeanie a couple of times before she and Alan had married. Jeanie had worked as his grandmother's part-time assistant while she was on the island. On the odd times he'd met her she'd been quiet, he remembered, a shadow who'd seemed to know her place. He'd hardly talked to her, but she'd seemed...suitable. A suitable assistant for his grandmother.

And then Alan had married her. What a shock and what a disaster—and Jeanie had been into it up to her neck.

Until today he'd seen her as a money-grubbing mouse. The fire in her eyes now suggested the mouse image might possibly be wrong.

'Jeanie, this isn't about looking after—'

'Don't Jeanie me.' She glowered and went back to rubbing butter. 'I'm Mrs McBride. I'm Duncairn's housekeeper for the next few weeks and then I'm nothing to do with you.'

'Then we've both lost.'

'I told you, I've lost nothing. The castle's my place of employment, nothing more.'

'So you wouldn't mind moving to Edinburgh?'

Her hands didn't even pause. She just kept rubbing in the already rubbed-in butter, and her glower moved up a notch.

'Don't talk nonsense. I'm moving nowhere.'

'But you *are* moving out of the castle.'

'Which is none of your business.'

'I'm offering you a job.'

'I don't want a job.'

'If you don't have the castle, you need a job.'

'Don't mess with me, Alasdair McBride. By the way, the kitchen's out of bounds to guests. That's what you are now. A guest. The estate's in the hands of the executors, and I'm employed here. You have a bed booked for the night. The library, the dining room and your bedroom and sitting room are where you're welcome. Meanwhile I have work to do.'

'Jeanie…'

'What?' She pushed the bowl away from her with a vicious shove. 'Don't play games with me, Alasdair. Your cousin messed with my life and I should have moved away then. Right away.'

'I want to help.'

'No, you don't. You want your inheritance.'

'Yes,' he said and he lost it then, the cool exterior he carefully presented to the world. 'Yes, I do. The Duncairn financial empire is colossal and far-reaching. It's also my life. To break it up and use it to fund dogs' homes…'

'There are some very deserving dogs,' she

snapped and then looked under the table to where Eileen's two dopey spaniels lay patiently waiting for crumbs. 'These two need a home. You can provide for them first.'

'Look!' He swore and hauled his phone from his sporran—these things were a sight more useful than pockets—and clicked the phone open. He flicked through a few screens and then turned it to face her. 'Look!'

'I have flour on my hands.' She glowered some more and she looked…sulky. Sulky but cute, he thought, and suddenly he found himself thinking…

Um…no. Not appropriate. All this situation needed was a bit of sensual tension and the thing was shot. He needed to stay calm, remember who she was and talk sense.

'Just look,' he said patiently and she sighed and rubbed her hands on her apron and peered at the screen.

'What am I looking at?'

'At a graph of Duncairn's listed charitable donations made in the last financial year,' he told her. 'The figure to the left represents millions. It scrolls off the screen but you can see the biggest beneficiaries. My grandfather and my grandmother after him refused to make Duncairn a listed company, so for years now the profits have either been siphoned back into the company to expand our power base, or used to fund worthwhile projects. AIDS, malaria, smallpox… Massive health projects have all been beneficiaries. Then there are smaller projects. Women's refuges, otter conservation, even dogs' homes.'

And Jeanie seemed caught. 'Those bars are… millions?' she whispered.

'Millions.'

'Then what was Eileen thinking, to leave the lot to just one cause?'

'You know what she was thinking,' Alasdair said wearily. 'We both do. She was blackmailing us into marriage, and as far as I can see, she's succeeded. I have no choice.' He sighed. 'The value of the castle ought to be enough for you, but if it's not, I'll pay you what you ask. I'll mortgage what I have to. Is that what you're after? You can name your terms but look at the alternative to us both. Use your head. I have no expectations of you, and I'll expect nothing from you as my wife. Eileen's will says we have to share a house for one full year before the inheritance is finalised, but I have a huge place in Edinburgh.

I'll fund you well enough so you can be independent. Jeanie, do this, if not for the charities I represent, then for you. You'll earn even more than the castle this way. You've won. I concede. We'll marry and then we'll move on.'

And then he stopped. There was no more argument to present.

There was total silence and it lasted for a very long time.

Marriage…

Third-time lucky? The thought flashed through her mind and she put it away with a hollow, inward laugh. Lucky? With this man?

What he was proposing was purely business. Maybe that was the way to go.

This was a marriage for sensible, pragmatic reasons, she told herself, fighting desperately for logic. She could even feel noble, saving the Duncairn billions for the good of all the charities it assisted.

Noble? Ha. She'd feel sullied. Bought.

He thought she'd walk away with a fortune. If he only knew… But there was no point in telling him about the bankruptcy hanging over her head.

'Would you like to see through the place in

Edinburgh?' he said at last. 'It's good, and big enough for us never to see each other. I'll have contracts drawn up that'll give you a generous income during the year, and of course we'll need a prenuptial agreement.'

'So I don't bleed you for anything else?'

'That wasn't what I was thinking.' But of course it was. It was an easy supposition—a woman who'd angled for the castle would no doubt think of marriage in terms of what she could get. 'But the castle will be worth—'

'Shut up and let me think.'

Whoa.

This woman was the hired help. She could see him thinking it. She was his cousin's leavings. The offer he'd made was extraordinary. That she would tell him to shut up…

He opened his mouth to reply, she glared—and he shut up.

More silence.

Could she? she thought. Dared she?

She thought suddenly of Maggie, her best friend on the island. Maggie was a fisherman's wife now, and the mother of two bright boys. Maggie was solid, sensible. She imagined Maggie's reaction when…if…she told her the news.

You're marrying another one? Are you out of your mind?

She almost grinned. It'd almost be worth it to hear the squeal down the phone.

But...

Act with your head. Do not be distracted, she told herself. You've done this in haste twice now. Get this right.

Marriage.

For a year. For only a year.

She'd have to live in Edinburgh, on Alasdair's terms.

No. Even the thought left her exposed, out of control, feeling as she'd vowed never to feel again. No and no and no.

She needed time to think, but that wasn't going to happen. Alasdair was leaning back, watching her, and she knew if she left this kitchen without making a decision the memory of this man would make her run. Physically, he was a stronger, darker version of Alan.

Alan had betrayed her, used her, conned her, but until that last appalling night he'd never frightened her. But this man... It was almost as if he were looking straight through her.

So leave, she told herself. It'd be easy, to do

what she'd first thought when the terms of the will were spelled out. She could stay with Maggie until she found a job.

A job, on Duncairn? There weren't any.

She glanced around her, at the great kitchen, at the big old range she'd grown to love, at the two dopey dogs at her feet. This place had been her refuge. She'd built it up with such care. Eileen had loved it and so had Jeanie.

It would have broken Eileen's heart if she'd known Alasdair was forced to let it go. Because of her? Because she lacked courage?

What if…? What if…?

'Think about it overnight,' Alasdair said, pushing himself away from the door. 'But I'm leaving in the morning. I need a decision by then.'

'I've made my decision.'

He stilled.

She'd poured the milk into the flour and turned it to dough without noticing. Now she thumped the dough out of the bowl and flattened it. She picked up her cutter and started cutting, as if perfectly rounded scones were the only thing that mattered in the world.

'Jeanie…'

She shook her head, trying to figure how to

say it. She finished cutting her scones, she re-formed and flattened the remaining dough, she cut the rest, she arranged them on the tray and then she paused.

She stared down at the scone tray. They were overworked, too. They wouldn't rise properly. She should give up now.

But she wouldn't give up. She'd loved Eileen. Okay, Eileen, you win, she told her silently and then she forced herself to look at the man before her.

'I'll do it if I can stay here,' she managed.

He didn't get it. He didn't understand where this was going, but business acumen told him not to rush in. To wait until she spelled out terms.

She was staring down at her scones. She put her hands on her waist and her head to one side, as if considering. She was considering the scones. Not him.

She had a tiny waist, he thought irrelevantly, for one so…curvy. She was wearing a tailored suit under her apron—for the funeral. Her suit had showed off her neat figure, but the tight ribbons of the apron accentuated it even more. She was curvy at the bottom and curvy at the top…

Um, very curvy, he conceded. Her hair was tied up in a knot but wisps were escaping.

She had a smudge of flour on her cheek. He'd like to…

Um, he wouldn't like. Was he out of his mind? This was business. Stick to what was important.

He forced himself to relax, walking forward so he had his back to the fire. Moving closer.

He felt rather than saw her flush.

Inexplicably, he still had the urge to remove that smudge of flour, to trace the line of her cheekbone, but the stiffening of her spine, the bracing of her shoulders, told him he might well get a face covered in scone dough for his pains.

'We'd need to live in Edinburgh,' he said at last, cautiously.

'Then there's not even the smidgeon of a deal.'

'Why the hell…?'

And at that she whirled and met his gaze full on, her green eyes flashing defiance. She was so close…

She was so angry.

'Once upon a time I ached to get off this island,' she snapped. 'Once upon a time I was a fool. The islanders—with the exception of my father—support and care for me. In Edinburgh I have no one. I'd be married to a man I don't know and I can't trust. I've married in haste before, Alasdair McBride, and I'll not do so again. You have much more to gain from this arrangement than I have, so here are my terms. I'll marry you for a year as long as you agree to stay in this castle. Then, at the end of the year, I'll inherit what the will has decreed I inherit. Nothing more. But meanwhile, you live in this castle—in my home, Alasdair—and you live on my terms for the year. It's that or nothing.'

'That's ridiculous.' He could feel her anger, vibrating in waves, like electric current, surging from her body to his and back again.

'Take it or leave it,' she said and she deliberately turned her back, deliberately broke the connection. She picked up her tray of unbaked scones and slid them into the trash. 'I'm trying again,' she told him, her back to him. 'Third-time lucky? It might work for scones.'

He didn't understand. 'I can't live here.'

'That's your decision,' she told him. 'But I have some very fine whisky I'm willing to share.'

'I'm not interested in whisky!' It was an explosion and Jeanie stilled again.

'Not?'

'This is business.'

'The whole year will be business,' she retorted, turning to the sink with her tray. 'I'm thinking it'll be shortbread for the guests tonight. What do you think?'

'I don't care what you give your guests.'

'But, you see, they'll be your guests, too, Lord Duncairn,' she told him. 'If you decide on marriage, then I'll expect you to play host. If you could keep wearing your kilt—a real Scottish lord playing host in his castle—I'll put you on the website. It'll pull the punters in in droves.'

'You're out of your mind.'

'And so was Eileen when she made that will,' Jeanie told him, still with her back to him. 'So all we can do is make the most of it. As I said, take it or leave it. We can be Lord and Lady of the castle together or we can be nothing at all. Your call, Lord Duncairn. I need to get on with my baking.'

CHAPTER THREE

FOUR WEEKS LATER Lord Alasdair Duncan Edward McBride, Sixteenth Earl of Duncairn, stood in the same kirk where his grandmother's funeral had taken place, waiting for his bride.

He'd wanted a register office. They both had. Jeanie was deeply uncomfortable about taking her vows in a church, but Eileen's will had been specific. Marriage in the kirk or nothing. Jeanie had felt ill when the lawyer had spelled it out, but then she'd looked again at the list of charities supported by the Duncairn foundation, she'd thought again of the old lady she'd loved, and she'd decided God would forgive her.

'It's not that I don't support dogs' homes,' she told Maggie Campbell, her best friend and her rock today. 'But I feel a bit of concern for AIDS and malaria and otters as well. I'm covering all bases. Though it does seem to the world like I'm buying myself a castle with marriage.' She hadn't told Maggie of the debt. She'd told no one. The whole island would think this deal would be her being a canny Scot.

'Well, no one's judging you if you are,' Maggie said soundly, hugging her friend and then adjusting the spray of bell heather in Jeanie's simple blue frock. 'Except me. I would have so loved you to be a bride.'

'I should have worn my suit. I'm not a bride. I'm half a contract,' Jeanie retorted, glancing at her watch and thinking five minutes to go, five minutes left when she could walk out of here. Or run. Honestly, what was she doing? Marrying another McBride?

But Maggie's sister was a lawyer, and Maggie's sister had read the fine print and she'd got the partners in her firm to read the fine print and then she'd drawn up a prenuptial agreement for both Jeanie and Alasdair to sign and it still seemed…sensible.

'This is business only,' she said aloud now, and Maggie stood back and looked at her.

'You look far too pretty to be a business deal. Jeanie, tomorrow you'll be the Lady of Duncairn.'

'I… He doesn't use the title.' She'd tried joking about that to Alasdair. She'd even proposed using it in castle advertising but the black look on his face had had her backing right off. You didn't joke with Lord Alasdair.

Just Alasdair. Her soon-to-be husband.

Her…lord?

'It doesn't stop the title being there, My Lady-ship.' Maggie bobbed a mock curtsy as she echoed Jeanie's thoughts. 'It's time to go to church now, m'lady. If m'lady's ready.'

Jeanie managed a laugh but even to her ears it sounded hollow. She glanced at her watch again. Two minutes. One.

'Ready, set, go,' Maggie said and propelled her to the door.

To marry.

Third-time lucky?

He was standing at the altar, waiting for his bride. He'd never thought he'd be here. Marriage was not for him.

He hadn't always believed that, he conceded. Once upon a time he'd been head over heels in love. He'd been twenty-two, just finishing a dou-ble degree in law and commerce, eager to take on the world. Celia had been a socialite, five years his senior. She was beautiful, intelligent, a woman who knew her way around Scottish society and who knew exactly what she wanted in a marriage.

He couldn't believe she'd wanted him. He'd been lanky, geeky, unsure, a product of cold parents and too many books, knowing little of how relationships worked. He'd been ripe for the plucking.

And Celia had plucked. When she'd agreed to marry him, he'd thought he was the luckiest man alive. What he hadn't realised was that when she was looking at him she was seeing only his title and his inheritance.

But she'd played her part superbly. She'd held him as he'd never been held. She'd listened as he'd told her of his childhood, things he'd never told anyone. He'd had fun with her. He'd felt light and free and totally in love. Totally trusting. He'd bared his soul, he'd left himself totally exposed— and in return he'd been gutted.

For a long time he'd blamed his cousin, Alan, with his charm and charisma. Alan had arrived in Edinburgh a week before he and Celia were due to marry, ostensibly to attend his cousin's wedding but probably to hit his grandmother for more money. He hadn't been involved with Jeanie then. He'd had some other bimbo on his arm, but that hadn't cramped his style. Loyalty hadn't been in Alan's vocabulary.

And it seemed it wasn't in Celia's, either.

Two days before his wedding, Alasdair had realised he'd left his briefcase at Celia's apartment. He'd had a key so he'd dropped by early, before work. He'd knocked, but of course no one had answered.

It was no wonder they hadn't answered. He'd walked in, and Celia had been with Alan. *With*, in every sense of the word.

So now he was about to marry…another of Alan's leavings?

Don't think of Alan now. Don't think of Celia. He said it savagely to himself but the memory was still sour and heavy. He'd never trusted since. His personal relationships were kept far apart from his business.

But here he was again—and he was doing what Celia had intended. Wedding for money?

This woman was different, he conceded. Very different. She was petite. Curvy. She wasn't the slightest bit elegant.

She was Alan's widow.

But right now she didn't look like a woman who'd attract Alan. She was wearing a simple blue frock, neat, nice. Her shoes were kitten-heeled, silver. Her soft brown curls were just brushing her shoulders. She usually wore her hair tied back or up, so maybe this was a concession to being a bride—as must be the spray of bell heather on her lapel—but they were sparse concessions.

Celia would have been the perfect bride, he thought tangentially. That morning, when he'd walked in on them both, Celia's bridal gown had been hanging for him to see. Even years later he still had a vision of how Celia would have looked in that dress.

She wouldn't have looked like this. Where Celia would have floated down the aisle, an ethereal vision, Jeanie was looking straight ahead, her gaze on the worn kirk floorboards rather than on him. Her friend gave her a slight push. She nodded as if confirming something in her mind—and then she stumped forward. There was no other word for it. She stumped.

A romantic bride? Not so much.

Though she was...cute, he conceded as he watched her come, and then he saw the flush of colour on her cheeks and he thought suddenly she looked...mortified?

Mortified? As if she'd been pushed into this?

It was his grandmother who'd done the forcing, he told himself. If this woman had been expecting the castle to fall into her lap with no effort, it was Eileen who'd messed with those plans, not him. This forced marriage was merely the solution to the problem.

And mortified or not, Jeanie had got what she wanted. She'd inherit her castle.

He'd had to move mountains to arrange things so he could stay on the island. He'd created a new level of management and arranged audits to ensure he hadn't missed anything; financial dealings would run smoothly without him. He'd arranged a satellite Internet connection so he could work here. He'd had a helipad built so he could organise the company chopper to get him here fast. So he could leave fast.

Not that he could leave for more than his designated number of nights, he thought grimly. He was stuck. With this woman.

She'd reached his side. She was still staring

stolidly at the floor. Could he sense…fear? He must be mistaken.

But he couldn't help himself reacting. He touched her chin and tilted her face so she had no choice but to meet his gaze.

'I'm not an ogre.'

'No, but—'

'And I'm not Alan. Business only.'

She bit her lip and his suspicion of fear deepened.

Enough. There were few people to see this. Eileen's lawyer was here to see things were done properly. The minister and the organist were essential. Jeanie's friend Maggie completed the party. 'I need Maggie for support,' Jeanie had told him and it did look as if she needed the support right now. His bride was looking like a deer trapped in headlights.

He took her hands and they were shaking.

'Jeanie…'

'Let's…let's…'

'Not if you're not sure of me,' he told her, gentling now, knowing this was the truth. 'No money in the world is worth a forced marriage. If you're afraid, if you don't want it, then neither do I. If you don't trust me, then walk away now.'

What was he saying? He was out of his mind. But he'd had to say it. She was shaking. Acting or not, he had to react to what he saw.

But now her chin was tilting in a gesture he was starting to recognise. She tugged her hands away and she managed a nod of decision.

'Eileen trusted you,' she managed. 'And this is business. For castle, for keeps.' She took a deep breath and turned to the minister. 'Let's get this over with,' she told him. 'Let's get us married.'

The vows they spoke were the vows that were spoken the world over from time immemorial, between man and woman, between lovers becoming man and wife.

'I, Alasdair Duncan Edward McBride, take thee, Jeanie Margaret McBride... To have and to hold. For richer or for poorer. In sickness and in health, for as long as we both shall live.'

He wished—fiercely—that his grandmother hadn't insisted on a kirk. The minister was old and faded, wearing Wellingtons under his well-worn cassock. He was watching them with kindly eyes, encouraging them, treating them as fresh-faced lovers.

For as long as we both shall live...

In his head he corrected himself.

For twelve months and I'm out of here.

For as long as we both shall live...

The words were hard to say. She had to fight to get her tongue around them.

It should be getting easier to say the words she knew were just words.

The past two times, she'd meant them. She really had.

They were nonsense.

Stupidly she felt tears pricking at the backs of her eyelids and she blinked them back with a fierceness born of an iron determination. She would not show this man weakness. She would not be weak. This was nothing more than a sensible proposition forced on her by a crazy will.

You understand why I'm doing it, she demanded silently of the absent Eileen. You thought you'd force us to become family. Instead we're doing what we must. You can't force people to love.

She'd tried, oh, she'd tried, but suddenly she was remembering that last appalling night with Alan.

'Do you think I'd have married you if my grandmother hadn't paid through the nose?'

Eileen was doing the same thing now, she thought bleakly. She was paying through the nose.

But I'm doing it for the right reasons. Surely? She looked firmly ahead. Alasdair's body was brushing hers. In his full highland regalia he looked…imposing. Magnificent. Frightening.

She would not be frightened of this man, she told herself. She would not. She'd marry, she'd get on with her life and then she'd walk away.

For as long as we both shall live…

Somehow she made herself say the words. How easy they'd been when she'd meant them but then they'd turned out to be meaningless. Now, when they were meaningless to start with, it felt as if something were dying within.

'You may kiss the bride,' the minister was saying and she felt like shaking her head, turning and running. But the old man was beaming, and Alasdair was taking her hands again. The new ring lay stark against her work-worn fingers.

Alasdair's strong, lean hands now sported a wedding band. Married.

'You may kiss the bride…'

He smiled down at her—for the sake of the

kindly old minister marrying them? Surely that was it, but, even so, her heart did a back flip. What if this was real? her treacherous heart said. What if this man really loved…?

Get over it. It's business.

But people were watching. People were waiting. Alasdair was smiling, holding her hands, ready to do what was right.

Kiss the bride.

Right. She took a deep breath and raised her face to his.

'Think of it like going to the dentist,' Alasdair whispered, for her ears alone, and she stared up at him and his smile widened.

And she couldn't help herself. This was ridiculous. The whole thing was ridiculous. Jeanie Lochlan marrying the Earl of Duncairn. For a castle.

She found herself chuckling. It was so ridiculous she could do it. She returned the grip on his hands and she even stood on tiptoe so he could reach her.

His mouth lowered onto hers—and he kissed her.

If only she hadn't chuckled. Up until then it had been fine. Business only. He could do this. He could marry her, he could keep his distance, he could fulfil the letter of the deal and he could walk away at the end of twelve months feeling nothing. He intended to feel nothing.

But that meant he had to stay impervious to what she was; to who she was. He couldn't think of her as his wife at all.

But then she chuckled and something happened.

The old kirk. The beaming minister. The sense of history in this place.

This woman standing beside him.

She was in this for profit, he told himself. She was sure of what she wanted and how she was going to get it. She was Alan's ex-wife and he'd seen how much the pair of them had cost Eileen. He wanted nothing to do with her.

But she was standing before him and he'd felt her fear. He'd felt the effort it had cost her to turn to the minister and say those vows out loud.

And now she'd chuckled.

She was small and curvy and dressed in a simple yet very pretty frock, with white lace collar, tiny lace shoulder puffs and a wide, flouncy skirt cinched in at her tiny waist. She was wearing bell heather on her lapel.

She was chuckling.

And he thought, She's enchanting. And then the thought flooded from nowhere.

She's my wife.

It hit him just as his mouth touched hers. The knowledge was as if a floodgate had opened. This woman...

His wife...

He kissed her.

She'd been expecting...what? A cursory brushing of lips against lips? Or less. He could have done this without actually touching her. That would have been better, she thought. An air kiss. No one here expected any more.

She didn't get an air kiss. He'd released her hands. He put his hands on her waist and he lifted her so her mouth was level with his.

He kissed her.

It was a true wedding kiss, a lordly kiss, the kiss of the Lord of Duncairn claiming his bride. It was a kiss with strength and heat and passion. It was a kiss that blew her fragile defences to smithereens.

She shouldn't respond. She shouldn't! They were in a kirk, for heaven's sake. It wasn't seemly.

This was a business arrangement, a marriage of convenience, and he had no right…

And then her mind shut down, just like that.

She'd never been kissed like this. She'd never felt like this.

Fire…

His mouth was plundering hers. She was raised right off her feet. She was totally out of control and there was nothing she could do but submit.

And respond? Maybe she had no choice. Maybe that was the only option because that was what her body was doing. It was responding and responding and responding.

How could it not? This was like an electric charge, a high-voltage jolt that had her locked to him and there was no escape. Not that she wanted to escape. The fire coursing through her body had her feeling…

Here was her home? Here was her heart?

This was nonsense. Crazy. Their tiny audience was laughing and cheering and she fought to bring them into focus. She fought desperately to gather herself, regain some decorum, and maybe Alasdair felt it because finally, finally he set her on her feet. But his dark eyes gleamed at her, and behind that smile was a promise.

This man was her husband. The knowledge was terrifying but suddenly it was also exhilarating. Where were smelling salts when a girl needed them? she thought wildly, and she took a deep, steadying breath and turned resolutely back to the minister. Get this over with, she pleaded silently, and let me get out of here.

But the Reverend Angus McConachie was not finished. He was beaming at her as a father might beam at a favourite daughter. In fact, the Reverend Angus had baptised her, had buried her mother, had caught her and her friends stealing strawberries from his vegetable patch, had been there for all her life. She'd tried to explain to him what this wedding was about but she doubted he'd listened. He saw what he wanted to see, the Reverend Angus, and his next words confirmed it.

'Before I let you go…' he was beaming as if he'd personally played matchmaker, and happy families was just beginning '… I wish to say a few words. I've known our Jeanie since the time she turned from a twinkle in her father's eye into a pretty wee bairn. I've watched her grow into the fine young woman she is today. I know the Lady Eileen felt the same pleasure and pride in her that I do, and I feel the Lady Eileen is looking down right now, giving these two her blessing.'

Okay, Jeanie thought. That'll do. Stop now. But this was the Reverend Angus and she knew he wouldn't.

'But it's been my sorrow to see the tragedies that have befallen our Jeanie,' the minister continued, his beam dipping for a moment. 'She was devoted to her Rory from the time she was a wee lass, she was a fine wife and when the marriage ended in tragedy we were all heartbroken for her. That she was brave enough to try again with her Alan was a testament to her courage—and, dare I say, it was also a testament to the Lady Eileen's encouragement? I dare say there's not an islander on Duncairn whose heart didn't break with her when she came home after such trouble.'

'Angus…' Jeanie hissed, appalled, but Angus's beam was back on high and there was no stopping him.

'And now it's three,' he said happily. 'Third-time lucky. I hear the Lady Eileen has her fingers in the pie this time, too, but she assured me before she died that this one would be a happy ever after.'

'She told you?' Alasdair asked, sounding incredulous.

'She was a conniving lass, your grandmother.' Angus beamed some more. 'And here it is, the results of that conniving, and the islanders couldn't be happier for you. Jeanie, lass, may third time be more than lucky. May your third time be forever.'

Somehow they made it outside, to the steps of the kirk. The church sat on the headland looking over Duncairn Bay. The sun was shining. The fishing fleet was out, but a few smaller boats were tied on swing moorings. Gulls were wheeling overhead, the church grounds were a mass of wild honeysuckle and roses, and the photographer for the island's monthly newsletter was asking them to look their way.

'Smile for the camera… You look so handsome, the pair of you.'

This would make the front cover of the *Duncairn Chronicle*, she knew—*Local Lass Weds Heir to Duncairn*.

Her father would be down in the pub now, she thought, already drinking in anticipation of profits he'd think he could wheedle from her.

'This is the third time?' Alasdair sounded incredulous.

'So?' Her smile was rigidly determined. Alasdair's arm was around her waist, as befitted the standard newlywed couple, but his arm felt like steel. There was not a trace of warmth in it.

'I assumed Alan was the only—'

'You didn't ask,' she snapped. 'Does it matter?'

'Hell, of course it matters. Did you make money from the first one, too?'

Enough. She put her hand behind her and hauled his arm away from her waist. She was still rigidly smiling but she was having trouble… it could so easily turn to rictus.

'Thanks, Susan,' she called to the photographer. 'We're done. Thanks, everyone, for coming. We need to get back to the castle. We have guests arriving.'

'No honeymoon?' Susan, the photographer, demanded. 'Why don't you go somewhere beautiful?'

'Duncairn is beautiful.'

'She won't even close the castle to guests for a few days,' Maggie said and Jeanie gritted her teeth and pushed the smile a bit harder.

'It's business as usual,' she told them. 'After

all, this is the third time I've married. I'm think-ing the romance has worn off by now. It's time to get back to work.'

Alasdair drove them back to the castle. He'd bought an expensive SUV—brand-new. It had been delivered via the ferry, last week before Alasdair had arrived. Alasdair himself had ar-rived by helicopter this morning, a fact that made Jeanie feel as if things were happening far too fast—as if things were out of her control. She'd been circling the SUV all week, feeling more and more nervous.

She wasn't a 'luxury-car type'. She wasn't the type to marry a man who arrived by helicopter. But she had to get used to it, she told herself, and she'd driven the thing down to the kirk feeling… absurd.

'It's gorgeous,' Maggie had declared. 'And he's said you can drive it? Fabulous. You can share.'

'This marriage isn't about sharing, and my little banger is twenty years old. She's done me proud and she'll keep doing me proud.'

'Och, but I can see you sitting up beside your husband in this, looking every inch the lady.'

Maggie had laughed and she'd almost got a swipe to the back of her head for her pains.

But now… She was doing exactly that, Jeanie thought. She was sitting primly in the front passenger seat with her hands folded on her lap. She was staring straight ahead and beside her was… her husband.

'Third time…'

It was the first time he'd spoken to her out of the hearing of their guests. As an opening to a marriage it was hardly encouraging.

'Um…' Jeanie wasn't too sure where to go.

'You've been married three times.' His mind was obviously in a repetitive loop, one that he didn't like a bit. His hands were clenched white on the steering wheel. He was going too fast for this road.

'Cattle and sheep have the right of way here,' she reminded him. 'And the cattle are tough wee beasties. You round a bend too fast and you'll have a horn through your windscreen.'

'We're not talking about cattle.'

'Right,' she said and subsided. His car. His problem.

'Three…' he said again and she risked a glance at his face. Grim as death. As if she'd conned him?

'Okay, as of today, I've been married three times.'

He was keeping his temper under control but she could feel the pressure building.

'Did my grandmother know?' His incredulity was like a flame held to a wick of an already ticking bomb.

But if he thought he had sole rights to anger, he had another thought coming. As if she'd deceive Eileen…

'Of course she knew. Eileen knew everything about me. I…loved her.'

And the look he threw her was so filled with scorn she flinched and clenched her hands in her lap and looked the other way.

Silence. Silence, silence and more silence. Maybe that's what this marriage will be all about, she thought bleakly. One roof, but strangers. Silence, with undercurrents of…hatred? That was what it felt like. As if the man beside her hated her.

'Was he rich, too?' Alasdair asked and enough was enough.

'Stop.'

'What…?'

'Stop the car this instant.'

'Why should I?'

But they were rounding a tight bend, where even Alasdair had to slow. She unclipped her seat belt and pushed her door wide. 'Stop now because I'm getting out, whether you've stopped or not. Three, two…'

He jammed on the brakes and she was out of the door before they were completely still.

He climbed out after her. 'What the…?'

'I'm walking,' she told him. 'I don't do dinner for guests but seeing you live at the castle now you can have the run of the kitchen. Make yourself what you like. Have a happy marriage, Alasdair McBride. Your dislike of me means we need to be as far apart as we can, so we might as well start now.'

And she turned and started stomping down the road.

She could do this. It was only three miles, and if there was one thing Jeanie had learned to do over the years, it was walk. She loved this country. She loved the wildness of it, the sheer natural beauty. She knew every nook and cranny of the island. She knew the wild creatures. The sheep hardly startled at her coming and she knew each of the highland cattle by name.

But she was currently wearing a floaty dress and heels. Not stilettos, she conceded, thanking her lucky stars, but they were kitten heels and she wasn't accustomed to kitten heels.

Maybe when Alasdair was out of sight she'd slip them off and walk barefoot.

Ouch.

Nevertheless, a girl had some pride. She'd made her bed and she needed to lie on it. Or walk.

She walked. There was no sound of an engine behind her but she wasn't looking back.

And then a hand landed on her shoulder and she almost yelped. Almost. A girl had some pride.

'Don't,' she managed and pulled away to keep stomping. And then she asked, because she couldn't help herself, 'Where did you learn to walk like a cat?'

'Deerstalking. As a kid. My grandpa gave me a camera for my eighth birthday.'

'You mean you don't have fifty sets of antlers on your sitting-room walls back in Edinburgh?' She was still stomping.

'Nary an antler. Jeanie—'

'Mrs McBride to you.'

'Lady Jean,' he said and she stopped dead and closed her eyes. *Lady Jean...*

Her dad would be cock-a-hoop. He'd be drunk by now, she thought, boasting to all and sundry that his girl was now lady of the island.

His girl.

Rory... She'd never been her father's girl, but Rory used to call her that.

'My lass. My sweet island lassie, my good luck charm, the love of my life...'

That this man could possibly infer she'd married for money...

'Go away,' she breathed. 'Leave me be and take your title and your stupid, cruel misconceptions with you.'

And she started walking again.

To her fury he fell in beside her.

'Go away.'

'We need to talk.'

'Your car's on a blind bend.'

'This is my land.'

'*Your* land?'

There was a moment's loaded pause. She didn't stop walking.

'Okay, *your* land,' he conceded at last. 'The access road's on the castle title. As of marrying, as of today, it's yours.'

'You get the entire Duncairn company. Does that mean you're a bigger fortune hunter than me?'

'I guess it does,' he said. 'But at least my motive is pure. How much of Alan's money do you have left?'

And there was another statement to take her breath away. She was finding it hard to breathe. Really hard.

Time for some home truths? More than time. She didn't want sympathy, but this…

'You'd think,' she managed, slowly, because each word was costing an almost superhuman effort, 'that you'd have done some homework on your intended bride. This is a business deal. If you're buying, Alasdair McBride, surely you should have checked out the goods before purchase.'

'It seems I should.' He was striding beside her. What did he think he was doing? Abandoning the SUV and hiking all the way to the castle?

'I have guests booked in at four this afternoon,' she hissed. 'They'll be coming round that bend. Your car is blocking the way.'

'You mean it's blocking your profits?'

Profits. She stopped mid-stride and closed her eyes. She counted to ten and then another ten. She tried to do a bit of deep breathing. Her fingers clenched and re-clenched.

Nothing was working. She opened her eyes and he was still looking at her as if she was tainted goods, a bad smell. He'd married someone he loathed.

Someone who married for profit... Of all the things she'd ever been accused of...

She smacked him.

She'd never smacked a man in her life. She'd never smacked anyone. She was a woman who used Kindly Mousers and carried the captured mice half a mile to release them. She swore they beat her back to the castle but still she kept trying. She caught spiders and put them outside. She put up with dogs under her bed because they looked so sad when she put them in the wet room.

But she had indeed smacked him.

She'd left a mark. *No!*

Her hands went to her own face. She wanted to sink into the ground. She wanted to run. Of all the stupid, senseless things she'd done in her life, this was the worst. She'd married a man who made her so mad she'd hit him.

She'd mopped up after Rory's fish for years. She'd watched his telly. She'd coped with the meagre amount he'd allowed her for housekeeping—and she'd never once complained.

And Alan... She thought of the way he'd treated her and still... She'd never once even considered hitting.

But now... What was she thinking? Of all the stupid, dumb mistakes, to put herself in a situation where she'd ended up violent...

Well, then...

Well, then what? A lesser woman might have burst into tears but not Jeanie. She wasn't about to show this man tears, no matter how desperate things were.

Move on, she told herself, forcing herself to think past the surge of white-hot anger. Get a grip, woman. Get yourself out of this mess, the fastest way you can. But first...

She'd smacked him and the action was indefensible. Do what comes next, she told herself. Apologise.

'I'm sorry.' Somehow she got it out. He was staring at her as if she'd grown two heads, and who could blame him? How many times had the Lord of Castle Duncairn been slapped?

Not often enough, a tiny voice whispered, but she wasn't going there. No violence, not ever. Had she learned nothing?

'I'm very sorry,' she made herself repeat. 'That was inexcusable. No matter what you said, I should never, ever have hit you. I hope… I hope it doesn't hurt.'

'Hurt?' He was still eyeing her with incredulity. 'You hit me and ask if it hurts? If I say no, will you do it again?' And it was almost as if he was goading her.

She stared at him, but her stare was blind.

'I won't…hit you.'

'What have I possibly said to deserve that?'

'You judged me.'

'I did. Tell me what's wrong about my judgement.'

'You want the truth?'

'Tell me something I don't know,' he said wearily and her hand itched again.

Enough. No more. Say it and get out.

He wanted the truth? He wanted something he didn't know? She took a deep breath and steadied.

Let him have it, then, she told herself. After all, the only casualty was her pride, and surely she ought to be over pride by now.

'Okay, then.' She was feeling ill, cold and empty. She hated what she was about to say. She hated everything that went with it.

But he was her husband, she thought bitterly. For now. For better or for worse she'd made the vows. The marriage would need to be annulled and fast, but meanwhile the truth was there for the telling. Pride had to take a back seat.

'I make no profit. I won't inherit the castle, no matter how married I am,' she told him. 'Believe it or not, I did this for you—or for your inheritance, for the Duncairn legacy Eileen cared so much about. But if I can't see you without wanting to hit out, then it's over. No lies are worth it, no false vows, no inheritance, nothing. I've tried my best but it's done.'

Done? The world stilled.

It was a perfect summer's day, a day for soaking in every ounce of pleasure in preparation for the bleak winter that lay ahead. But there was no pleasure here. There was only a man and a woman, and a chasm between them a mile deep.

Done.

'What do you mean?' he asked at last.

'I mean even if we managed to stay married for a year, I can't inherit,' she told him, in a dead, cold voice she scarcely recognised. 'I've checked with two lawyers and they both tell me the same thing. Alan left me with massive debts. For the year after his death I tried every way I could to figure some way to repay them but in the end there was only one thing to do. I had myself declared bankrupt.'

'Bankrupt?' He sounded incredulous. Did he still think she was lying? She didn't care, she decided. She was so tired she wanted to sink.

'That was almost three years ago,' she forced herself to continue. 'But bankruptcy lasts for three years and the lawyers' opinions are absolute. Because Eileen died within the three-year period, any inheritance I receive, no matter when I receive it, becomes part of my assets. It reverts to the bankruptcy trustees to be distributed between Alan's creditors. The fact that most of those creditors are any form of low-life you care to name is irrelevant. So that's it—the only one who stood to gain from this marriage was you. I agreed to marry you because I knew Eileen would hate the estate to be lost, but now...

Alasdair, I should never have agreed in the first place. I'm sick of being judged. I'm tired to death of being a McBride, and if it's driving me to hitting, then I need to call it quits. I did this for Eileen but the price is too high. Enough.'

She took off her shoes, then wheeled and started walking.

Where was a spacecraft when she needed one? 'Beam me up, Scotty…' What she'd give to say those words.

Her feet wouldn't go fast enough.

'Jeanie…' he called at last but she didn't even slow.

'Take your car home,' she threw over her shoulder. 'The agreement's off. Everything's off. I'll see a lawyer and get the marriage annulled—I'll do whatever I need to do. I'd agreed to look after the castle for the next few weeks but that's off, too. So sue me. You can be part of my creditor list. I'll camp in Maggie's attic tonight and I'm on the first ferry out of here tomorrow.'

'You can't,' he threw after her, sounding stunned, but she still didn't turn. She didn't dare.

'Watch me. When I reach the stage where I hit out, I know enough is enough. I've been enough of a fool for one lifetime. Foolish stops now.'

CHAPTER FOUR

THERE WAS ONE advantage to living on an island—there were only two ferries a day. Actually it was usually a disadvantage, but right now it played into Alasdair's hands. Jeanie might be heading to Maggie's attic tonight but she'd still be here in the morning. He had time.

He needed time. He needed to play catch up. Jeanie was right: if she'd been a business proposition, he would have researched before he invested.

An undischarged bankrupt? How had he not known? The complications made his head spin.

The whole situation made his head spin.

He tried to get her to ride home with him but she refused. Short of hauling her into the SUV by force he had to let her be, but he couldn't let her walk all the way. He figured that was the way to fuel her fury and she was showing enough fury as it was. He therefore drove back to the castle, found her car keys hanging on a nail in the kitchen, drove her car back along the track until he reached her, soundlessly handed her the keys, then turned and walked back himself.

She must have spent a good hour trying to figure out how not to accept his help, or maybe she didn't want to pass him on the track. Either way, he was back at the castle when her car finally nosed its way onto the castle sweep.

Maybe he should have talked to her then, but he didn't have all the facts. He needed them.

Luckily he had help, a phone call away.

'Find anything there is to find out about Jeanie Lochlan, born on Duncairn twenty-nine years ago,' he told his secretary. Elspeth was his right-hand woman in Edinburgh. If anyone could unearth anything, it was her.

'Haven't you just married her?' Elspeth ventured.

'Don't ask. Just look,' he snapped and whatever Elspeth heard in his voice he didn't care.

Jeanie was back in her rooms downstairs. He was in his sitting room right over hers. He could hear her footsteps going back and forth, back and forth. Packing?

Finally he heard her trudge towards the front door.

He met her at the foot of the castle stairs and tried to take an enormous suitcase from her.

'I can manage.' Her voice dripped ice. 'I can cope by myself.'

And what was it about those few words that made him flinch?

She was shoving her case into the back of her battered car and he was feeling as if...feeling as if...

As if maybe he'd messed something up. Something really important.

Yes, he had. He'd messed up the entire Duncairn empire, but right now it felt much more personal.

She closed the lid of the boot on her car and returned. He stood and watched as she headed for the kitchen, grabbed crates and wads of newspaper and headed for the library.

He followed and stood at the door as she wrapped and stowed every whisky bottle that was more than a third full.

The B & B guests would come back tonight and be shattered, he thought. Half the appeal of this place on the web was the simple statement:

'Genuine Scottish Castle, with every whisky of note that this grand country's ever made free to taste.'

He'd seen the website and had congratulated his grandmother on such a great selling idea.

'The whisky's Jeanie's idea,' Eileen had told him. 'I told her I thought the guests would drink themselves silly, but she went ahead and bought them anyway, out of her own salary. She lets me replenish it now, but the original outlay and idea were hers. So far no one's abused it. The guests love it, and you're right, it's brilliant.'

And the guests were still here. They'd want their whisky.

'And don't even think about claiming it,' she snapped as she wrapped and stowed. 'I bought the first lot out of my wages so it's mine. Be grateful I'm only taking what's left. Alasdair, you can contact Maggie if you want my forwarding address…for legalities. For marriage annulment. For getting us out of this final foolishness. Meanwhile that's it. I'm done and out of here. From this day forth I'm Jeanie Lochlan, and if I never see a McBride again, it'll be too soon.'

She picked up her first crate of whisky and

headed to the car. Silently he lifted the second and carried it after her.

She shoved both crates into the back seat and slammed the door after them. Her little car shuddered. It really was a banger, he thought.

Alan's wife. An undischarged bankrupt. Alan… He thought of his cousin and he felt ill.

'Jeanie, can we talk?'

'We've talked. Goodbye.' She stuck out her hand and waited until he took it, then shook it with a fierceness that surprised him. Then she looked up at his face, gave one decisive nod and headed for the driver's seat.

'I'm sorry about the castle,' she threw at him. She could no longer see him. She was hauling on her seat belt, moving on. 'And I'm sorry about your company. On the upside, there are going to be some very happy dogs all over Europe.'

He stood and watched her as she headed out of the castle grounds, along the cliff road towards the village. When she disappeared from view he watched on.

His entire financial empire had just come crashing down. He should be gutted.

He was gutted but what was uppermost in his

mind right now was that he'd hurt her. She'd hit him but the next moment she'd drawn back as if he'd been the one who'd hit her.

He had made assumptions, he thought, but those assumptions had been based on facts. He knew how much money Eileen had withdrawn from the company when Jeanie and Alan had married. 'It'll set them up for life,' Eileen had told him. 'I know Alan's not interested in the company but he is my grandson. He wants his inheritance now, and if it helps him settle, then he should have it.'

The amount she'd given the pair had been eye-watering. And yes, Alan's lifestyle had been ruinous but his death must have meant most of the capital was intact. Surely Alan couldn't have gambled that much?

Surely?

He'd always thought Jeanie's decision to come back here to the castle was an attempt to ingratiate herself with his grandmother. The contents of Eileen's will had proved him right.

The sight of her heading away in her ancient car gave him pause.

An undischarged bankruptcy…

If it was true, then the castle was forfeit no matter whether they married or not.

And with that thought came another. He'd loved the castle since he was a child, even when it was little more than a ruin. Eileen's restoration had made it fabulous. She'd been overwhelmingly proud of it—and so was he. He gazed up now at the turrets and towers, the age-old battlements, the great, grand home that had sheltered so many generations of his family. That had provided work for so many islanders…

He was the Lord of Duncairn. Even though he no longer used it, the title, but the castle and the island were still important to him. Desperately important. With her leaving, Jeanie had sealed the castle's fate. It would leave the family forever.

He was forcing his mind to think tangentially. If what she'd just told him was based on facts, then it wasn't Jeanie who'd sealed the castle's fate. It had been Alan.

He thought suddenly of the night Alan had been killed. He'd been driving a brand-new sports car, far too fast. A clear road. An inexplicable swerve to the left, a massive tree.

Jeanie had been thrown clear, suffering minor injuries. Alan had died instantly.

He'd thought until now it had been alcohol or drugs that had caused the crash, but now... Had it been suicide? Because of debt?

Had he tried to take Jeanie with him?

He'd been too caught up with Eileen's grief to ask questions. What sort of fool had he been?

A car was approaching, a low-slung, crimson sports car. The couple inside wore expensive clothes and designer sunglasses. The car spun onto the driveway, sending up a spray of gravel. The pair climbed out, looking at the castle in awe.

And they also looked at Alasdair. He was still in his wedding finery. Lord of his castle?

He'd lose the castle. Alan had gambled it away.

And he'd gambled more than the castle away. Jeanie... He'd gambled with her life.

'Hi, there.' The young man was clearly American, and he was impervious to the fact that Alasdair's gaze was still following Jeanie's car. He flicked the boot open and pointed to the baggage, then turned back to his partner. 'This looks cool,' he told her. 'And check out the doorman. Great touch.' And he tossed the car keys to Alasdair, who was so stunned that he actually caught them.

'This is just what we ordered—real Scotland,' he continued. 'Wow, look at those ruins down by the sea. You can put them on the Internet, honey. And check out the battlements. I've half a mind to put in an offer for the place, doorman and all. But first, my love, let's check out this whisky.' He glanced back at Alasdair. 'What are you waiting for, man? We need our bags straight away.'

'Carry your own bags,' Alasdair snapped. 'I don't work in this place. I own it.'

Only he didn't.

'As far as short marriages go, this must be a record.'

Down in the village, Maggie had chosen a top-of-the-range bottle from Jeanie's crates and had poured two whiskies. They were sitting at Maggie's kitchen table, surrounded by the clutter of Maggie's kids, Maggie's fisherman husband and the detritus of a busy family. The ancient stove was giving out gentle warmth but Jeanie couldn't stop shaking. Maggie's hug had made her feel better, the whisky should be helping, but she had a way to go before shock lessened.

'So the marriage lasted less than an hour,' Maggie continued. 'I'm guessing…not consummated?'

'Maggie!'

'Just asking.' Maggie grinned and raised her glass. 'You might need to declare that to get an annulment—or am I thinking of the bad old days when they checked the sheets?'

'I can hardly get a doctor to declare me a virgin,' Jeanie retorted, and Maggie's smile broadened. But behind her smile Jeanie could see concern. Real concern.

'So what happened? Did he come on too fast? Is he a brute? Tell me.'

If only, Jeanie thought, and suddenly, weirdly, she was thinking of her mother. Heather Lochlan had died when Jeanie was sixteen and Jeanie still missed her with an ache that would never fade.

'He's not a brute. He's just...a businessman.' She buried her face in her hands. 'Mam would never have let me get myself into this mess,' she whispered. 'Three husbands... Three disasters.'

'Your mam knew Rory,' Maggie retorted. 'Rory was no disaster. Your mam would have danced at your wedding.'

She well might have, Jeanie thought. Rory had been an islander, born and bred. He'd been older than Jeanie by ten years, and he'd followed his father and his grandfather's way to the sea. He'd been gentle, predictable, safe. All the things Jeanie's dad wasn't.

She'd been a mere sixteen when her dad had taken control of her life.

Her mam's death had been sudden and shocking, and Jeanie's dad had turned to drink to cope. He'd also pulled Jeanie out of school. 'Sixteen is well old enough to do the housework for me. I'm wasting no more of my money.'

She'd been gutted, but then Rory had stepped in, and amazingly he'd stood up to her father. 'We'll marry,' he'd told her. 'You can work in the fish shop rather than drudge for your father. You can live with my mam and dad.'

Safe... That was what Rory was. She'd thought she loved him, but...

But working in the fish shop, doing an online accountancy course because she ached to do something other than serve fish and clean, waiting for the times Rory came home from sea, fitting in with Rory's life...sometimes she'd dreamed...

It had never come to a point where she'd chafed against the bonds of loving, for Rory had drowned. She'd grieved for him, honestly and openly, but she knew she should never have married him. Safety wasn't grounds for a marriage. She'd found a part-time job with the island solicitor, and she'd begun to think she might see London. Maybe even save for a cruise…

But it had been so hard to save. She'd still been cleaning for her in-laws. She'd been earning practically nothing. Dreams had seemed just that— dreams. And then Eileen had come and offered her a job, acting as her assistant whenever she was on the island. And with Eileen… Alan.

Life had been grey and drab and dreary and he'd lit up everything around him. But…

There was that *but* again.

'Mam would have told me not to be a fool,' she told Maggie. 'Maybe even with Rory. Definitely with Alan and even more definitely with this one.'

'Maybe, but a girl has to follow her heart.'

'My heart doesn't make sense. I married Rory for safety. I married Alan for excitement. I married…this one…so he could keep his inheritance. None of them are the basis for any sort of marriage. It's time I grew up and accepted it.'

'So what will you do now?' Maggie was watching her friend with concern.

'I'm leaving the island. I never should have

come back after Alan's death. I was just…so homesick and battered, and Eileen was kind.' She took a deep breath. 'No matter. I've enough money to tide me over for a few weeks and there are always bookkeeping jobs.' She raised her whisky to her friend. 'Here's to an unmarried future,' she said.

'Och,' Maggie exclaimed, startled. 'You can't expect me to drink to that.'

'Then here's to an unmarried Jeanie Lochlan,' Jeanie told her. 'Here's to just me and that's how it should be. I'm on my own and I'm not looking back.'

Alasdair was not on his own. He was surrounded by eight irate guests and two hungry dogs. Where did Jeanie keep the dog food? He had no idea.

He'd stayed in the castle off and on when his grandmother was ill, and after his grandmother's funeral. During that time the castle had been full of women and casseroles and offers of help. Since that time, though, he'd been back in Edinburgh, frantically trying to tie up loose ends so he could stay on the island for twelve months. He'd arrived this morning via helicopter, but the helicopter was long gone.

He was stuck here for the night, and the castle was full, not with offers of help, but with eight guests who all wanted attention.

'Where's the whisky, fella? We only came for the whisky.' That was the American, growing more and more irate.

'Jeanie has shortbread.' That was the shorter of two elderly women in hiking gear. 'I'm Ethel, and Hazel and I have been here a week now. We know she made it, a big tin. Hazel and I ate three pieces each last night, and we're looking forward to more. If you could just find it… Oh, and Hazel needs a hot-water bottle. Her bunion's playing up. I told her she should have seen the doctor before she came but would she listen? She's ready for a drop of whisky, too. When did you say Jeanie would be back?'

He'd assumed Jeanie had some help. Someone other than just her. These people were acting as if Jeanie were their personal servant. What the…?

'I'll ring the village and get whisky delivered,' he said and the American fixed him with a death stare.

'That's not good enough, man. It should be here now.'

'We've had a problem.'

'Is something the matter with Jeanie?' The lady called Ethel switched to concern, closely followed by visions of disaster. 'Where is she? And the whisky? You've lost it? Were you robbed? Is Jeanie hurt? Oh, she's such a sweetheart. If anything happened to her, we'd never forgive ourselves. Hazel, Jeanie's been hurt. Oh, but if it's robbery, should we stay here…?'

'It's not robbery.'

'It'll be that father of hers,' Hazel volunteered. 'He came when we were here last year, blustering his way in, demanding money. He took her whisky. Oh, she'll be mortified, poor lass.'

'But where's *our* whisky?' the American demanded and Hazel swung around and raised her purse.

'If you say one more word about whisky when our Jeanie's in trouble, this'll come down on your head,' she told him. 'My bunion's killing me and I could use something to hit. Meanwhile Mr… Mr…' She eyed Alasdair with curiosity.

'McBride,' Alasdair told her.

And with the word, the elderly lady's face sagged into relief. 'You're family? Oh, we're so glad. Ethel and I worry about her being here in this place all alone. We didn't know she had any-one. Is she really all right?'

'I… Yes. She just…needs to stay in the village tonight. For personal reasons.'

'Well, why shouldn't she?' the lady demanded. 'All the times we've stayed here, we've never known her to take a night off, and she works so hard. But we can help. The doggies need their dinner, don't you, doggies? And we can make our own hot-water bottles. If you light the fire in the sitting room, Ethel and I will feed the dog-gies and find the shortbread. Oh, and we'll take the breakfast orders, too, so you'll have them all ready.' Her face suddenly puckered. 'But if Jeanie's not back by the morning…Ethel and I come for Jeanie's porridge. We can cope without whisky but not without our porridge.'

The guests headed to the village for dinner, and by the time they returned Alasdair had whisky waiting. It wasn't enough to keep the Americans happy, but the couple had only booked for one night and for one night Alasdair could cope with bluster.

But one night meant one morning. Breakfast. Ethel and Hazel had handed him the menus, beaming confidence. He'd glanced through them and thought there was nothing wrong with toast.

He couldn't cope with breakfast—and why should he? This marriage farce was over. All he had to do was accept it. He could contact the chopper pilot, get him here first thing and be back in Edinburgh by mid-morning.

He'd be back in charge of his life—but Hazel and Ethel wouldn't get their porridge and the Duncairn empire was finished.

He glanced again at the menus. Porridge, gourmet omelettes, black pudding...Omelettes were easy, surely. Didn't you just break eggs into a pan and stir? But black pudding! He didn't know where to start.

Did Jeanie do it all? Didn't she have anyone to help?

The memory flooded back of Jeanie in the car. What had he said to her? That his car was... *'blocking your profits...'*

The moment he'd said it he'd seen the colour drain from her face. The slap had shocked her more than it had shocked him.

An undischarged bankruptcy?

He didn't know anything about her.

What had she said? *'This is a business deal.*

If you're buying, Alasdair McBride, surely you should have checked out the goods.'

He'd set Elspeth onto a background check. Yes, he should have done it weeks ago but he'd assumed…

Okay, he'd assumed the worst—that Jeanie was as money-grubbing as her ex-husband. It had just seemed a fact.

He thought back to the one time—the only time—he'd seen Jeanie together with Alan. They'd just married. Alan had brought his new bride to the head offices of the Duncairn Corporation and introduced her with pride.

'Isn't she gorgeous?' he'd demanded of Alasdair and Alasdair had looked at Jeanie's short, short skirt and the leather jacket and boots and the diamond earrings and he'd felt nothing but disgust. The demure secretary he'd seen working with Eileen had been a front, he'd thought. The transformation made him wonder just how much his grandmother had been conned.

He was about to find out. 'You know what this means,' Alan had told him. 'I'm respectable now. The old lady thinks the sun shines out of Jeanie. She's already rethinking the money side of this business. Half this company should be mine and you know it. Now Eileen's thinking it, too.'

Eileen hadn't been thinking it, but she had settled an enormous amount on the pair of them. 'It's easier than to have the inheritance of the company split when I die, and Jeanie's excellent with money. She'll manage it.'

The next time he'd seen Jeanie, she'd been back here and his grandmother had been dying. There'd been no sign of the tight-fitting clothes or the jewels then. There'd been no sign of the brittle, would-be sophisticate—and there'd been no sign of the money.

On impulse he headed upstairs to the room his grandmother had kept as her own. Eileen had spent little time here but when she'd known her time was close she'd wanted to come back. He had to clear it out—sometime. Not now. All he wanted to do now was look.

He entered, wincing a little at the mounds of soft pillows, at the billowing pink curtains, at the windows open wide to let in the warm evening air. Jeanie must still be caring for it. All signs of the old lady's illness had gone but the room was still Eileen's. Eileen's slippers were still beside the bed.

There were two photographs on the dresser. One was of him, aged about twelve, holding his first big salmon. He looked proud fit to burst. The other was of Alan and Jeanie on their wedding day.

Jeanie was holding a posy of pink roses. She was wearing a dress similar to the one she had on today. Alan was beaming at the camera, hugging Jeanie close, his smile almost…triumphant.

Jeanie just looked embarrassed.

So the tarty clothes had come after the wedding, he thought.

So the marriage to Alan had been almost identical to the one she'd gone through today?

Maybe it was. After all, he was just another McBride.

He swore and crossed to Eileen's desk, feeling more and more confused. The foundations he'd been so sure of were suddenly decidedly shaky.

What he was looking for was front and centre—a bound ledger, the type he knew Eileen kept for every transaction she had to deal with. This was the castle ledger, dealing with the day-to-day running of the estate. Jeanie would have another one, he knew, but, whatever she did, Eileen always kept a personal account.

He flicked through until he found the payroll.

Over the past couple of months there'd been a few on the castle staff. There'd been nurses, help from the village, the staff Alasdair had seen when he'd come to visit her. But before that...

Leafing through, he could find only two entries. One was for Mac, the gillie. Mac had been gillie here for fifty years and must be close to eighty now. He was still on full wages, though he must be struggling.

The castle wasn't running as a farm. The cattle were here mostly to keep the grass down, but still... He thought of the great rhododendron drive. It had been clipped since the funeral. There was no way Mac could have done such a thing, and yet there was no mention of anyone else being paid to do it.

Except Jeanie? Jeanie, who was the only other name in the book? Jeanie, who was being paid less than Mac? Substantially less.

What was a good wage for a housekeeper? He had a housekeeper in Edinburgh and he paid her more than this—to keep house for one man.

His phone rang. Elspeth.

'That was fast,' he told her, but in truth he was starting to suspect that what she had to find was easy. He could have found it out himself, he thought. His dislike of Alan had stopped him enquiring, but now… Did he want to hear?

'I thought I'd catch you before you start enjoying your wedding night,' Elspeth said and he could hear her smiling. 'By the way, did you want more of those financial records sent down? I'm not sure what you're worried about. If you tell me, I can help look.'

'I'm not worried about the business right now,' he growled and heard Elspeth's shocked silence. What a statement!

But she regrouped fast. She was good, was Elspeth. 'I've been busy but this has been relatively simple,' she told him. 'From what I've found there's nothing to get in the way of having a very good time. No criminal record. Nothing. There's just one major hiccup in her past.'

And he already knew it. 'Bankruptcy?'

'You knew?'

'I… Yes.' But how long for? Some things weren't worth admitting, even to Elspeth. 'But not the details. Tell me what you have. As much as you have.'

'Potted history,' she said. Elspeth had worked for him for years and she knew he'd want facts fast. 'Jeanie Lochlan was born twenty-nine years ago, on Duncairn. Her father is supposedly a fisherman, but his boat's been a wreck for years. Her mother sounds like she was a bit of a doormat.'

'Where did you get this information?' he demanded, startled. This wasn't facts and figures.

'Where does one get all local information?' He could hear her smiling. 'The post office is closed today, so I had to use the publican, but he had time for a chat. Jeanie's mother died when she was sixteen. Her father proceeded to try to drink himself to death and he's still trying. The local view is that he'll be pickled and stuck on the bar stool forever.'

So far he knew…well, some of this. He knew she was local. 'So…' he said cautiously.

'When she was seventeen Jeanie got a special dispensation to marry another fisherman, an islander called Rory Craig,' Elspeth told him. 'I gather she went out with him from the time her mam died. By all reports it was a solid marriage but no kids. She worked in the family fish shop until Rory drowned when his trawler sank. She was twenty-three.'

And that was more of what he hadn't known

about. The details of the first marriage. He'd suspected…

He'd suspected wrong.

'I guess she wouldn't be left all that well-off after that marriage,' he ventured and got a snort for his pains.

'Small family fishing business, getting smaller. The trawler sank with no insurance.'

'How did you get all this?' he demanded again.

'Easy,' Elspeth said blithely. 'I told the publican I was a reporter from Edinburgh and had heard Lord Alasdair of Duncairn was marrying an islander. He was happy to tell me everything—in fact, I gather the island's been talking of nothing else for weeks. Anyway, Rory died and then she met your cousin. You must know the rest.'

'Try me.'

'You mean you don't?'

'Eileen didn't always tell me…' In fact, she'd never told Alasdair anything about Alan. There'd been animosity between the boys since childhood and Eileen had walked a fine line in loving both. 'And Jeanie keeps herself to herself.'

'Okay. It seems your gorgeous cousin visited the island to visit his gran—probably to ask for money, if the company ledgers are anything to go by. He met Jeanie, he took her off the island and your grandmother paid him to marry her.'

'I...beg your pardon?'

'I'm good,' she said smugly. 'But this was easy, too. I asked Don.'

Don.

Alasdair had controlled the day-to-day running of the firm for years now, but Don had been his grandparents' right-hand man since well before Alasdair's time. The old man still had a massive office, with the privileges that went with it. Alasdair had never been overly fond of him, often wondering what he was paid for, but his place in his grandparents' affections guaranteed his place in the company, and gossip was what he lived for.

'So Don says...' Elspeth started, and Alasdair thought, This is just more gossip, I should stop her—but he didn't. 'Don says soon after Alan met Jeanie, he took her to Morocco. Eileen must have been worried because she went to visit—and Alan broke down and told her the mess he was in. He was way over his head, with gambling debts that'd make your eyes water. He'd gone to the castle to try to escape his creditors—that's when he met Jeanie—and then he'd decided to go back to Morocco and try to gamble his way out of trouble. You can imagine how that worked. But he hadn't told Jeanie. She still had stars in her eyes—so Eileen decided to sort it.'

'How did she sort it?' But he already knew the answer.

'I'd guess you know.' Elspeth's words echoed his thoughts. 'That was when she pulled that second lot of funds from the company, but she gave it to Alan on the understanding that no more was coming. She was sure Jeanie could save him from himself, and of course Alan made promise after promise he never intended to keep. I'm guessing Eileen felt desperate. You know how she loved your cousin, and she saw Jeanie as the solution. Anyway, after his death Eileen would have helped Jeanie again—Don says she felt so guilty she made herself ill—but Jeanie wouldn't have any of it. She had herself declared bankrupt. She accepted a minimal wage from Eileen to run the castle, and that's it. End of story as far as Don knows it.' She paused. 'But, Alasdair, is this important? And if it is, why didn't you ask Don before you married her? Why didn't you ask *her*?'

Because I'm stupid.

No, he thought grimly. It wasn't that. He'd known Alan gambled. He knew the type of people Alan mixed with. If he'd enquired… If he'd known for sure that Jeanie was exactly the same as Alan was, with morals somewhere between a sewer rat and pond scum, he'd never have been able to marry her.

Except he had believed that. He'd tried to suppress it, for the good of the company, for the future of the estate, but at the back of his mind he'd branded her the same as he'd branded Alan.

'She still married him,' he found himself muttering. How inappropriate was it to talk like this to his secretary about…his wife? But he was past worrying about appropriateness. He was feeling sick. 'She must have been a bit like him.'

'Don said Eileen said she was a sweet young thing who was feeling trapped after her husband died,' Elspeth said. 'She was working all hours, for Eileen when your grandmother was on the island but also for the local solicitor, and cleaning in her husband's family's fish shop as well. Being paid peanuts. Trying to pay off the debt left after her husband's trawler sank with no insurance. She was bleak and she was broke. Don thinks Alan simply seduced her off the island. You know how charming Alan was.'

He knew.

He sat at the chair in front of Eileen's dresser and stared at himself in the mirror. The face that looked back at him was gaunt.

What had he done?

'But it's lovely that you've married her,' Elspeth said brightly now. 'Doesn't she deserve a happy ending? Don said she made Eileen's last few months so happy.'

She had, he conceded. He'd been a frequent visitor to the castle as his grandmother neared the end, and every time he'd found Jeanie acting as nursemaid. Reading to her. Massaging her withered hands. Just sitting…

And he'd thought… He'd thought…

Yeah, when the will was read he'd expected Jeanie to be mentioned.

That was what Alan would have done—paid court to a dying woman.

'Is there anything else you need?' Elspeth asked.

Was there anything else he needed? He breathed out a few times and thought about it.

'Yes,' he said at last.

'I'm here to serve.' He almost smiled at that.

Elspeth was fifty and bossy and if he pushed her one step too far she'd push back again.

'I need a recipe for black pudding,' he told her.

'Really?'

'Really.'

'I'll send it through. Anything else?'

'Maybe a recipe for humble pie as well,' he told her. 'And maybe I need that first.'

CHAPTER FIVE

MIDNIGHT. THE WITCHING HOUR. Normally Jeanie was so tired that the witches could do what they liked; she couldn't give a toss. Tonight the witches were all in her head, and they were giving her the hardest time of her life.

'You idiot. You king-size madwoman. To walk back into the McBride realm…'

Shut up, she told her witches, but they were ranting and she lay in the narrow cot in Maggie's tiny attic and held her hands to her ears and thought she was going mad.

Something hit the window.

That'll be more witches trying to get in, she told herself and buried her head under the pillow.

Something else hit the window. It sounded like a shower of gravel.

Rory used to do this, so many years ago, when he wanted to talk to her and her father was being…her father.

The ghost of Rory? That's all I need, she

thought, but then another shower hit the window and downstairs Maggie's Labrador hit the front door and started barking, a bark that said terrorists and stun grenades were about to launch through the windows and a dog had to do its duty. Wake up and fight, the dog was saying to everyone in the house. No, make that everyone in the village.

There was an oath from Maggie's husband in the room under Jeanie's, and, from the kids' room, a child began to cry.

And she thought...

No, she didn't want to think. This was nothing to do with her. She lay with her blanket pulled up to her nose as she heard Maggie's husband clump down the stairs and haul the door open.

'What do you think you're doing?' Dougal's shout was as loud as his dog's bark. 'McBride... It's McBride, isn't it? What the hell...? You might be laird of this island, but if you think you can skulk round our property... You've woken the bairns. Shut up!' The last words were a roar, directed at the dog, but it didn't work the way Dougal intended. From under her window came a chorus of frenzied barks in response.

Uh-oh. Jeanie knew those barks. Abbot and

Costello! Alasdair was here and he'd brought Eileen's dogs for the ride.

And then it wasn't just Maggie's dog and Eileen's dogs. The neighbours' dog started up in response, and then the dogs from the next house along, and then the whole village was erupting in a mass of communal barking.

Lights were going on. Maggie's two kids were screaming. She could hear a child start up in the house next door.

Should I stay under the pillows? Jeanie thought. It had to be the wisest course.

'I need to speak to my wife.' It was Alasdair, struggling to make himself heard above the din.

His wife. She needed more pillows—the pillows she had didn't seem to be effective.

'Jeanie?' That was Maggie, roaring up the stairs. 'Jeanie!'

'I'm asleep!'

'Jeanie, you know how much I love you, but your man's roaring in the street and he's woken the bairns. Either you face him or I will, and if it's me, it won't be pretty.'

Alasdair wasn't roaring in the street, Jeanie thought helplessly, but everyone else was. Everyone in Duncairn would know that the Earl of

Duncairn was under Maggie's window—wanting his wife.

Everyone knew everything on this island, she thought bitterly as she hauled on jeans and a sweatshirt and headed downstairs. Why broadcast more? As if the whole mess wasn't bad enough... She didn't want to meet him. She did not. She'd had enough of the McBrides to last her a lifetime.

Dougal was still in the doorway, holding the dog back. He'd stopped shouting, but as she appeared he looked at her in concern. 'You sure you want to go out there, lass?'

She glowered. 'Maggie says I have to.'

There was a moment's pause while they both thought about it. 'Then better to do what Maggie says,' he said at last. Dougal was a man of few words and he'd used most of them on Alasdair. 'Tell him to quiet the dogs. I'll be here waiting. Any funny business and I'm a call away. And don't be going out there in bare feet.'

Her shoes were in the attic, two flights of stairs away. At home...at the castle...she always left a pair of wellies at the back door, but here it hadn't been worth her unpacking.

The only Wellingtons on the doorstep were Dougal's fishing boots.

But a girl had to do what a girl had to do. She shoved her feet into Dougal's vast fishing wellies and went to meet her…her husband.

He'd found out where Maggie lived. That had been easy—the island boasted one slim phone book with addresses included. He hadn't meant or wanted to wake the house but she'd told him she'd be sleeping in the attic. All he'd wanted was for her to put her head out to investigate the shower of stones, he'd signal her down and they could talk.

The plan hadn't quite worked. Now the whole village was waiting for them to talk, and the village wasn't happy. But as a collective, the village was interested.

'Have you run away already, love?' The old lady living over the road from Maggie's was hanging out of the window with avid interest. 'Well, it's what we all expected. Don't you go letting him sweet-talk you back to his castle. Just because he's the laird… There's generations of lairds had their way with the likes of us. Don't you be trusting him one inch.'

She might not be trusting him, he thought, but at least she was walking towards him. She was wearing jeans, an oversize windcheater and huge fishermen's boots. Her curls were tumbled around her face. By the light of the street lamp she looked young, vulnerable…and scared.

Heck, he wasn't an ogre. He wasn't even really a laird. 'Jeanie…'

'You'd better hush the dogs,' she told him. 'Why on earth did you bring them?'

'Because when I tried to leave they started barking exactly as they're barking now.' He needed to be calm, but he couldn't help the note of exasperation creeping in. 'And your guests have already had to make do with half a shelf of whisky instead of a full one, and bought biscuits instead of home-made. What did you do with the shortbread? If the dogs keep barking, we'll have the castle empty by morning.'

'Does that matter?' But she walked across to the SUV and yanked open the door. 'Shush,' she said. They shushed.

It was no wonder they shushed. Her tone said don't mess with me and the dogs didn't. She was small and cute and fierce—and the gaze she turned on him was lethal.

She glowered and then hesitated, glancing up at the lit window over the road. 'It's all right, Mrs McConachie, I have him… I have things under control. Sorry for the disturbance, people. You can all go back to bed now. Close your windows, nothing to see.'

'You tell him, Jeanie,' someone shouted, and there was general laughter and the sound of assorted dogs faded to silence again.

But she was still glowering. She was looking at him as if he were five-day-old fish that had dared infiltrate the immaculate castle refrigerators.

Speaking of food… Why not start off on neutral territory?

'I don't know how to make black pudding,' he told her and her face stilled. The glare muted a little, as if something else was struggling to take its place. Okay. Keep it practical, he told himself, and he soldiered on. 'Two of your guests, Mr and Mrs Elliot from Battersea, insist they want black pudding for their breakfast. And Ethel and Hazel want porridge.'

'Hector and Margaret adore their black pudding,' she said neutrally, and he thought, Excellent, this was obviously the way to lead into the conversation they had to have.

'So how do you make it?'

'I don't. Mrs Stacy on the north of the island makes them for me and she gets her blood from the island butcher. I have puddings hanging in the back larder. You slice and fry at need. The shortbread's on top of the dresser—I put it where I can't reach it without the step stool because otherwise I'll be the size of a house. The porridge is more complicated—you need to be careful not to make it lumpy but there are directions on the Internet. I'm sure you can manage.'

'I can't.'

'Well, then…' She stood back, hands on her hips, looking as if he was a waste of space for admitting he couldn't make porridge. 'That's sad, but the guests need to find somewhere else as a base to do their hill climbing. They might as well get disgusted about their lack of black pudding and porridge tomorrow, and start looking elsewhere immediately.'

Uh-oh. This wasn't going the way he'd planned. She looked as if she was about to turn on her heels and retreat. 'Jeanie, there was a reason you agreed to marry me.' He needed to get things back on a sensible course now. 'Believe it or not, it's still the right thing to do. It was a good decision. You can't walk away.'

'The decision to marry? The right thing?'

'I believe it still is, even though…even though your reasons weren't what I thought they were. But long-term, it still seems sensible.'

'It did seem sensible.' She still sounded cordial, he thought, which had to be a good sign, or at least she still seemed neutral. But then she continued: 'But that was before I realised you think I'm a gold-digging harpy who's spent the last three years sucking up to Eileen so I can inherit the castle. Or maybe I did know that, but it got worse. It was before you inferred I'd married twice for money, three times if you count marrying you. You thought I was a tart the first time you saw me and—'

'I didn't.'

'Come off it. When Alan introduced us you looked like you'd seen lesser things crawl out of cheese. I concede the way I was dressed might have swayed you a little—'

'A little!' He still remembered how he'd felt as Alan had ushered her into his office. Appalled didn't begin to cut it.

'Alan said it was a joke,' she told him, a hint

of defensiveness suddenly behind her anger. 'He said you were a judgemental prude, let's give you a heart attack. He said you were expecting him to marry a tart so let's show him one. I was embarrassed to death but Alan wanted to do it and I was naïve and I thought I was in love and I went along with it. It even seemed…funny. It wasn't funny, I admit. It was tacky. But Alan was right. You were judgemental. You still are. Eileen kept telling me you were nice underneath but then she loved Alan, too. So now I've been talked into doing something against my better judgement—again. It has to stop and it's stopping now. I'll get the marriage annulled. That's it. If you don't mind, my bed's waiting and you have oats to soak. Or not. Lumpy porridge or none at all, it's up to you. I don't care.'

And she turned and walked away.

Or she would have walked away if she hadn't been wearing men's size-thirteen Wellington boots. There was a rut in the pavement, her floppy toe caught and she lurched. She flailed wildly, fighting for balance, but she was heading for asphalt.

He caught her before she hit the ground. His

arms went round her; he swung her high into his arms and steadied. For one moment he held her—he just held.

She gasped and wriggled. He set her on her feet again but for that moment...for that one long moment there'd been an almost irresistible urge to keep right on holding.

In the olden days a man could choose a mate according to his status in the tribe, he thought wryly. He could exert a bit of testosterone, show a little muscle and carry his woman back to his cave. Every single thing about that concept was wrong, but for that fleeting moment, as he held her, as he felt how warm, how slight, how yielding her body was, the urge was there, as old as time itself.

And as dumb.

But she'd felt it, too—that sudden jolt of primeval need. She steadied and backed, her hands held up as if to ward him off.

Behind them the door swung open. Dougal was obviously still watching through the window and he'd seen everything. 'You want me to come out, love?'

'It's okay, Dougal.' She sounded as if she was

struggling for composure and that made two of them. 'I…just tripped in your stupid wellies.'

'They're great wellies.' That was Maggie, calling over Dougal's shoulder. 'They're special ones I bought for his birthday. They cost a fortune.'

'I think they're nice, too,' Alasdair added helpfully and she couldn't help but grin. She fought to turn it back into a glower.

'Don't you dare make me laugh.'

'I couldn't.'

'You could. Go away. I'm going to bed.'

Enough. He had to say it. 'Jeanie, please come back to the castle,' he said, pride disappearing as the gravity of the next few moments hit home. 'You're right, I've been a judgemental fool. I've spent the last few hours trawling through Eileen's financial statements. I can see exactly what she has and hasn't given you. I can see what a mess Alan left you in. I can see…what you've given Eileen.'

She stilled. 'I don't know what you mean.'

'For the last three years you've made this castle a home for her,' he told her. 'I know Eileen's official home was in Edinburgh, and she still spent too much time in the office, trying to keep her fingers on the company's financial affairs.

But whenever she could, she's been here. When she became ill she was here practically full-time, only returning to Edinburgh long enough to reassure me there was no need for me to keep an eye on her. I thought she was staying here because she needed to keep an eye on you. I thought this was simply another financial enterprise. But tonight I spent a little time with your guests and some rather good whisky—'

'I didn't leave any good stuff behind.'

'I made an emergency dash. I spent a little time with them and they talked about why they've come back every year since you started running the B & B. They talked about how they and my grandmother talked about you and they talked about fun. How you and Eileen enjoyed each other's company, but that they'd always been welcome to join you. How Eileen sat in the library like a queen every night and presided over the whisky and talked about the estate as it's been, about my grandfather's ancestors and hers. It seems it didn't matter how often they heard it, they still loved it. And they talked about you, Jeanie, always in the background, always quietly careful that Eileen didn't do too much, that she didn't get cold, that she didn't trip on her stupid dogs. And then I looked at the wages and saw how little you've been paid. And Elspeth...'

'Who's Elspeth?' She sounded winded.

'My secretary. I asked her to do some long-overdue background checks. With the information you gave me this afternoon the rest was easy to find. She tells me that, as well as almost killing you that last night in his unpaid-for sports car, Alan died in debt up to his ears. He left you committed to paying them, even though most of them were to gambling houses and casinos. But somehow you seem to have become jointly responsible. I know Eileen would have paid them off, but they were vast debts, eye-watering debts, and you refused to let her help. You declared yourself bankrupt and then you accepted a minimal wage to stay on at the castle.'

'You have—'

'Been learning. Yes, I have. I've learned that this marriage arrangement gives you one more year in the castle but that's all it gives you. I'm still not sure why you agreed to marry me, but I'm pathetically grateful you did. Jeanie, I'm so sorry I misjudged you. Please come home.'

'It's not my home.'

'It is a home, though,' he said, gently now.

'That's what I didn't get. You made it Eileen's home and for that I can never thank you enough.'

'I don't want your thanks. Eileen let me stay. That was enough.'

'And I know I don't have the right, but I'm asking you to stay longer.'

'But not as your wife.'

'Legally as my wife. We both know that's sensible.'

'I don't do…sensible. I'm not very good at it. I have three dumb marriages to prove it.'

'Then do gut instinct,' he told her. 'Do what you think's right. Think back to the reasons you married me in the first place.'

'That's blackmail again.'

'It's not. I know I stand to gain a fortune by this transaction. You stand to gain nothing. That's what I hadn't understood. But we can work things out. If the company ends up in my name, I can buy the castle from the bankruptcy trustees. I intended to buy it from you anyway, but I can arrange for you to be paid more—'

'I don't want anything,' she snapped. 'Don't you get it? Don't you understand that there's nothing you can offer me that I want?'

'You do want another year in the castle. At the end of the year—'

'Don't even say it,' she told him. 'I will not be bought.'

Silence. What else could he say?

He could fix things if she let him. Duncairn Enterprises was extensive enough to soak up the purchase of the castle at market price. He could also settle a substantial amount on Jeanie when her bankruptcy was discharged, but he knew instinctively that saying that now would count for nothing. Right now, he had enough sense to know it would make things worse.

This woman—*his wife*—had married for a reason. She knew the good the company did. She knew how much the castle and the company meant to Eileen. He just had to hope those reasons were still strong enough.

'Jeanie, do you really want to get on that ferry tomorrow?' he asked. 'The dogs want you back at the castle. The guests want you. This does seem like cutting off your nose to spite your face. Please?'

'So…it's not just the porridge.'

'Not even the black pudding.'

'Alasdair…'

'There'll be no strings,' he said and held up his hands. 'I promise. Things will be as you imagined them when you agreed to this deal. You'll have a year's employment. You can use the year to sort what you want to do next and then you can walk away. There'll be no obligation on either of our parts.'

'No more insults?'

'I won't even comment on your footwear.'

She managed to smile again at that. It was faint but it was there.

And then there was silence. It was so deep and so long that Dougal opened the door again. He stood uncertainly on the doorstep. He made to say something but didn't. The silence lengthened. Finally he was dragged inside again by Maggie.

Maggie, at least, must understand the value of silence, Alasdair thought. The last light went off inside. Even if, as Alasdair suspected, Maggie was still lurking, she was giving them the pretence that they were alone.

The night was still and warm. The numbers of nights like this on Duncairn could be counted on less than a man's fingers. Everyone should be out tonight, he thought. The stars were hanging brilliant in the sky, as if they existed in a separate universe from the stars he struggled to see back in Edinburgh. The tide was high and he could hear the waves slapping against the harbour wall. Before dawn the harbour would be a hive of activity as the island's fishermen set to sea, but for now the village had settled back to sleep. There was no one here but this woman, standing still and watchful.

Trying to make her mind up whether to go or stay.

'Can I have the dogs?' she said at last, and he blinked.

'The dogs?'

'At the end of the year. That's been the thing that's hurt most. I haven't had time to find a job where I can keep them, and I can't see them living in an apartment in Edinburgh with you. If I stay, I'll have twelve months to source a job where they can come with me.'

'You'd agree to keeping on with the marriage,' he said, cautiously because it behoved a man to be cautious, 'for the dogs?'

'What other reason would there be?'

'For the company? So Duncairn Enterprises will survive?'

'That's your reason, not mine. Dogs or nothing, My Lord.'

'Don't call me that.'

She tilted her chin. 'I need something to hold on to,' she said. 'I need the dogs.'

He stared around at the two dogs with their heads hanging out of the window. Abbot was staring down at the road as if considering jumping. He wouldn't. Alasdair had been around this dog long enough to know a three-foot jump in Abbot's mind constituted suicide.

A moth was flying round Costello's nose. Costello's nose was therefore circling, too, as if he was thinking of snapping. He wouldn't do that, either. Risk wasn't in these two dogs' make-up and neither was intelligence.

'They're dumb,' he said, feeling dumbfounded himself.

'I like dumb. You know where you are with dumb. Dumb doesn't leave room for manipulation.'

'Jeanie…'

'Dumb or not, it's yes or no. A year at the castle, no insults, the dogs—and respect for my privacy. The only way this can work is if you keep out of my way and I keep out of yours.'

'We do still need to share the castle.'

'Yes, we do,' she agreed. 'But you'll be treated as a guest.'

'You mean you'll make the porridge?'

Her expression softened a little. 'I kind of like making it,' she admitted.

'So we have a deal?'

'No more insults?' she demanded.

'I can't think of a single insult to throw.'

'Then go home,' she told him. 'I'll be there before breakfast.'

'Won't you come back now?'

'Not with you,' she said flatly. 'I'll follow separately, when I'm ready. From now on, Alasdair McBride, this is the way we do things. Separately or not at all.'

How was a man to sleep after that? He lay in the great four-poster bed in the opulent rooms his grandmother had done up for him during the renovation and he kept thinking…of Jeanie.

Why hadn't his grandmother told him of her plight?

Because he'd never asked, he conceded. Eileen had known of the bad blood between the cousins. Revealing the mess Alan had left Jeanie in would have meant revealing even more appalling things of Alan than he already knew.

So she'd let him think Jeanie was a gold-digger?

No. Eileen wouldn't have dreamed he'd think Jeanie was mercenary, he conceded, because any-one who met Jeanie would know that such a thing was impossible.

Except him. He'd met her, he'd judged her and he'd kept on judging her. He'd made the offer of marriage based on the assumption that she was out for what she could get, and he'd nearly de-stroyed his chances of success in doing it.

Worse, he'd hurt her. He'd hurt a woman who'd done the right thing by Eileen. A woman Eileen had loved. A woman who'd agreed to a marriage because…because he'd told her of the charities Duncairn supported? Because she could spend another year acting as a low-paid housekeeper? Because she loved two dopey dogs?

Or because she'd known Eileen would have wanted him to inherit. The realisation dawned as clear as if it were written in the stars.

She'd done it for Eileen.

Eileen had loved her and he could see why. She was a woman worthy of…

Loving?

The word was suddenly there, front and centre, and it shocked him.

Surely he was only thinking of it in relation to Eileen—but for the moment, lying back in bed in the great castle of his ancestors, he let the concept drift. Why had Eileen loved her?

Because she was kind and loyal and warmhearted. Because she loved Eileen's dogs—why, for heaven's sake? Because she was small and cute and curvy and her chuckle was infectious.

There was nothing in that last thought that would have made Eileen love her, he decided, but it surely came to play in Alasdair's mind.

When she'd almost fallen, when he'd picked her up and held her, he'd felt...he'd felt...

As if she was his wife?

And so she was, he thought, and maybe it was the vows he'd made in the kirk so few hours ago that made him feel like this. He'd thought he could make them without meaning them, but now...

She was coming back here. His wife.

And if he made one move on her, she'd run a mile. He knew it. Alan had treated her like dirt and so had he. Today he'd insulted her so deeply that she'd run. This year could only work if it was business only.

He had to act on it.

There was a whine under the bed and Abbot slunk out and put his nose on the pillow. The dogs should be sleeping in the wet room. That was where their beds were but when he'd tried to lock them in they'd whined and scratched and finally he'd relented. Were they missing Jeanie?

He relented a bit more now and made the serious mistake of scratching Abbot's nose. Within two seconds he had two spaniels draped over his bed, squirming in ecstasy, then snuggling down and closing their eyes very firmly—*We're asleep now, don't disturb us.*

'Dumb dogs,' he told them but he didn't push them off. They'd definitely be missing Jeanie, he thought, and he was starting—very strongly—to understand why.

Why was she heading back to the castle? She was out of her mind.

But she'd packed her gear back into her car and now she was halfway across the island. Halfway home?

That was what the castle felt like. Home. Except it wasn't, she told herself. It had been her refuge after the Alan disaster. She'd allowed Eileen to talk her into staying on, but three years were three years too many. She'd fallen in love with the place. With Duncairn.

With the Duncairn estate and all it entailed?

That meant Alasdair, she reminded herself, and she most certainly hadn't fallen in love with Alasdair. He was cold and judgemental. He'd married her for money, and he deserved nothing from her but disdain.

But he'd caught her when she'd fallen and he'd felt…he'd felt…

'Yeah, he'd felt like any over-testosteroned male in a kilt would make you feel,' she snapped out loud.

Her conversation with herself was nuts. She had the car windows open and she'd had to stop. Some of the scraggy, tough, highland sheep had chosen to snooze for the night in the middle of the road. They were moving but they were taking their time. Meanwhile they were looking at her curiously—listening in on her conversation? She needed someone to talk to, she decided, and the sheep would do.

'I'm doing this for your sakes,' she told them.

'If I go back to the castle, he can buy it from the bankruptcy trustees at the end of the year and it'll stay in the family.'

Maybe he'll let me stay on as caretaker even then?

That was a good thought, but did she want to stay as housekeeper/caretaker at Duncairn for the rest of her life?

'Yes,' she said out loud, so savagely that the sheep nearest her window leaped back with alarm.

'No,' she corrected herself, but maybe that was the wrong answer, too. That was the dangerous part of her talking. That was the part of her that had chafed against being part of Rory's family business, doing the books, cleaning the fish shop, aching to get off the island and do something exciting.

Well, she had done something exciting, she told herself bitterly. She'd met and married Alan and she'd had all the excitement a girl could want and more.

'So it's back in your box to you, Jeanie McBride,' she told herself and thought briefly about her name. Jeanie McBride. She was that. She was Alan's widow.

She was Alasdair's wife.

'At the end of the year I'm going back to being Jeanie Lochlan,' she told the last sheep as it finally ambled off the road. 'Meanwhile I'm going back to being housekeeper at Duncairn, chief cook and bottle washer for a year. I'm going back to taking no risks. The only thing that's changed for the next twelve months is that the house has one permanent guest. That guest is Alasdair McBride but any trouble from him and he's out on his ear.'

And you'll kick him out how?

'I won't need to,' she told the sheep. 'I hold all the cards.

'For a year,' she reminded herself, wishing the sheep could talk back. 'And for a year...well, Alasdair McBride might be the Earl of Duncairn but he's in no position to lord it over me. For the next year I know my place, and he'd better know his.'

CHAPTER SIX

ALASDAIR WOKE AT DAWN to find the dogs had deserted him. That had to be a good sign, he told himself, but he hadn't heard Jeanie return.

His room was on the ocean side of the castle. The massive stone walls would mean the sound of a car approaching from the land side wouldn't have woken him.

That didn't mean she was here, though.

He wanted—badly—to find out. The future of Duncairn rested on the outcome of the next few minutes but for some reason he couldn't bear to know.

He opened his laptop. He didn't even know if she'd returned but it paid a man to be prepared.

It paid a man to hope?

By eight o'clock he'd formed a plan of action. He'd made a couple of phone calls. He'd done some solid work, but the silence in the castle was starting to do his head in. He couldn't put it off any longer. He dressed and headed down the great staircase, listening for noise—listening for Jeanie?

He pushed open the door to the dining room and was met by…normal. Normal?

He'd been in this room often but this morning it was as if he were seeing it for the first time. Maybe it was because last night he'd almost lost it—or maybe it was because this morning it was the setting for Jeanie. Or he hoped it was.

Regardless, it was some setting. The castle after Eileen's amazing restoration was truly luxurious, but Eileen—and Jeanie, her right-hand assistant—had never lost sight of the heart of the place. That heart was displayed right here. The massive stone fireplace took half a wall. A fire blazed in the hearth, a small fire by castle standards but the weather was warm and the flame was there mostly to form a heart—and maybe to form a setting for the dogs, who lay sprawled in front of it. Huge wooden beams soared above. The vast rug on the floor was an ancient design, muted yet glorious, and matching the worn floorboards to perfection.

There were guests at four of the small tables, the guests he'd given whisky to last night. They gave him polite smiles and went back to their breakfast.

Porridge, he thought, checking the tables at a glance. Black pudding. Omelettes!

Jeanie *must* be home.

And almost as he thought it, there she was, bustling in from the kitchen, apron over her jeans, her curls tied into a bouncy ponytail, her face fixed into a hostess-like beam of welcome.

'Good morning, My Lord. Your table is the one by the window. It has a fine view but the morning papers are beside it if you prefer a broader outlook. Can I fetch you coffee while you decide what you'd like for your breakfast?'

So this was the way it would be. Guest and hostess. Even the dogs hadn't stirred in welcome. Jeanie was home. They had no need of him.

Things were back to normal?

'I just need toast.'

'Surely not. We have eggs and bacon, sausages, porridge, black pudding, omelettes, pancakes, griddle cakes…whatever you want, My Lord, I can supply it. Within reason, of course.' And she pressed a menu into his hands and retreated to the kitchen.

* * *

He ate porridge. No lumps. Excellent.

He felt…extraneous. Would he be served like this for the entire year? He'd go nuts.

But he sat and read his paper until all the guests had departed, off to tramp the moors or climb the crags or whatever it was that guests did during their stay. The American couple departed for good, for which he was thankful. The rest were staying at least another night. Jeanie was obviously supplying picnic baskets and seeing each guest off on their day's adventures. He waited a few moments after the last farewell to give her time to catch her breath, and then headed to the kitchen to find her.

She was elbow deep in suds in front of the sink. Washed pots and pans were stacked up to one side. He took a dishcloth and started to dry.

'There's no need to be doing that.' She must have heard him come in but she didn't turn to look at him. 'Put the dishcloth down. This is my territory.'

'This year's a mutual business deal. We work together.'

'You've got your company's work to be doing.

There's a spare room beyond the ones you're using—your grandmother set it up as a small, private library for her own use. It has a fine view of the sea. We'll need to see if the Internet reaches there—if not you can get a router in town. Hamish McEwan runs the electrical store in Duncairn. He'll come out if I call him.'

Business. Her voice was clipped and efficient. She still hadn't looked at him.

'We need to organise more than my office,' he told her. 'For a start, we need a cleaning lady.'

'We do not!' She sounded offended. 'What could be wrong with my cleaning?'

'How many days a year do you take guests?'

'Three-sixty-five.' She said it with pride and scrubbed the pan she was working on a bit harder.

'And you do all the welcoming, the cooking, the cleaning, the bed-making...'

'What else would I do?'

'Enjoy yourself?'

'I like cleaning.'

'Jeanie?'

'Yes.'

'That pan is so shiny you can see your face in it. It's time you stopped scrubbing.'

There were no more dishes. He could see her

dilemma. She needed to stop scrubbing, but that would mean turning—to face him?

He lifted the pan from her hands, set it down and took her wet hands in his.

'Jeanie…'

'Don't,' she managed and tugged back but he didn't let her go.

'Jeanie, I've just been on the phone to Maggie.'

She stilled. 'Why?'

'To talk to her about you. You didn't tell her you were coming back here. She thought you'd gone to the ferry.'

He didn't tell her what a heart-sink moment that had been. She didn't need emotion getting in the way of what he had to say now.

'I thought I'd ring her this morning.' She sounded defensive. 'I thought… To be honest, when I left Maggie's I wasn't sure where I was going. I headed out near the ferry terminal and sat and looked over the cliffs for a while. I wasn't sure if I should change my mind.' She looked down at their linked hands. 'I'm still not sure if I should.'

'You promised me you'd come back.'

'I stood in the kirk and wed you, too,' she said

sharply. 'Somewhere along my life I've learned that promises are made to be broken.'

'I won't break mine.'

'Till death do us part?'

'I'll rethink that in a year.'

'You have to be kidding.' She wrenched her hands back with a jerk. 'It's rethought now. Promises mean nothing. Now if you'll excuse me, I have beds to make, a castle to dust, dogs to walk, then the forecourt to mow. You go back to sorting your electrics.'

'Jeanie, it's the first day of our honeymoon.'

'Do you not realise I'm over honeymoons?' She grabbed the pan he'd just taken from her and slammed it down on the bottom shelf so hard it bounced. 'What were you thinking? A jaunt to a six-star hotel with a casino on the side? Been there, done that.'

'I thought I'd take you out to see the puffins.'

And that shocked her. She straightened. Stared at him. Stared at him some more. 'Sorry?'

'Have you seen the puffins this year?'

'I... No.'

'Neither have I. I haven't seen the puffins since my grandfather died, and I miss them. According to Dougal, they're still there, but only just. You know they take off midsummer? Their breeding season's almost done so they'll be leaving any minute. The sea's so calm today it's like a lake. You have all the ingredients for a picnic right here and Dougal says we can use his *Mary-Jane*.'

'Dougal will lend you his boat?'

'It's not his fishing boat. It's just a runabout.'

'I know that, but still…he won't even trust Maggie with his boat.'

'Maybe I come with better insurance than Maggie.'

'Do you even know how to handle a boat?'

'I know how to handle a boat.'

She stared at him, incredulous, and then shook her head. 'It's a crazy idea. As I said, I have beds—'

'Beds to make. And dusting and dog-walking and grass to mow.' He raised his fingers and started ticking things off. 'First, beds and general housework. Maggie's mam is already on her way here, bringing a friend for company. They'll clean and cook a storm. They're bringing Maggie's dog, too, who Maggie assures me keeps Abbot and Costello from fretting. They'll walk all the dogs. Maggie's uncle is bringing up the rear. He'll do the mowing, help Mac check the cattle, do anything on the list you leave him. He'll be here in an hour but we should be gone by then. Our boat's waiting. Now, can I help you pack lunch?'

'No! This is crazy.'

'It's the day after your wedding. It's not crazy at all.'

'The wedding was a formality. I told you, I don't do honeymoons.'

'Or six-star hotels, or casinos. I suspected not. I also thought that if I whisked you off the island you might never come back. But, Jeanie, you do need a holiday. Three years without a break. I don't know what Eileen was thinking.'

'She knew I wouldn't take one.'

'Because you're afraid?' he said gently. He didn't move to touch her. In truth, he badly wanted to but she was so close to running… 'Because you've ventured forth twice and been burned both times? I know you agreed to marry so I could inherit, but there's also a part of you that wants another year of safe. Jeanie, don't you want to see the puffins?'

'I…'

'Come with me, Jeanie,' he said and he couldn't help himself then, he did reach out to her. He touched her cheek, a feather-light touch, a trace of finger against skin, and why it had the power to make him feel…make him feel…

As if the next two minutes were important. Really important. Would she pull away and tell him to get lost, or would she finally cut herself some slack? Come play with him…

'I shouldn't,' she whispered, but she didn't pull back.

'When did you last see puffins?'

She didn't reply. He let his hand fall, though it took effort. He wanted to keep touching. He wanted to take that look of fear from her face.

What had they done to her? he wondered. Nice, safe Rory, and low-life Alan…

There was spirit in this woman and somehow it had been crushed.

And then he thought of the slap and he thought, No, it hadn't quite been crushed. Jeanie was still under there.

'Not since I was a little girl,' she admitted. 'With my mam. Rory's uncle took us out to see them.'

'Just the once?'

'I… Yes. He took tourists, you see. There were never places—or time—to take us.'

What about your own dad? he wanted to ask. Jeanie's father was a fisherman. He'd had his own boat. Yes, it was almost two hours out to the isolated isles, the massive crags where the puffins nested, but people came from all over the world to see them. To live here and not see...

His own grandparents had taken him out every summer. When he'd turned sixteen they'd given him a boat, made sure he had the best instruction, and then they'd trusted him. When his grandfather had died he'd taken Eileen out there to scatter his ashes.

'Come with me,' he said now, gently, and she looked up at him and he could see sense and desire warring behind her eyes.

'It's not a honeymoon.'

'It's a day trip. You need a holiday so I'm organising a series of day trips.'

'More than one!'

'You deserve a month off. More. I know you won't take that. You don't trust me and we're forced to stay together and you don't want that, but for now...you've given me an amazing gift, Jeanie Lochlan. Allow me to give you something in return.'

She compressed her lips and stared up at him, trying to read his face.

'Are you safe to operate a boat out there?' she demanded at last.

'You know Dougal. Do you think he'd lend me the *Mary-Jane* if I wasn't safe?'

Dougal's uncle had taught him how to handle himself at sea. Once upon a time this island had been his second home, his refuge when life with his parents got too bad, and sailing had become his passion.

'He wouldn't,' Jeanie conceded. 'So we're going alone?'

'Yes.' He would have asked Dougal to take them if it would have made Jeanie feel safer but this weather was so good every fisherman worth his salt was putting to sea today. 'You can trust me, Jeanie. We're interested in puffins, that's all.'

'But when you touch me, I feel…'

And there it was, out in the open. This *thing* between them.

'If we're to survive these twelve months, we need to avoid personal attraction,' he told her.

Her face stilled. 'You feel it, too.'

Of course I do. He wanted to shout it, but the wariness in her eyes was enough to give a man pause. That and reason. Hell, all they needed was a hot affair, a passionate few weeks, a massive split, and this whole arrangement would be blown out of the water. Even he had the sense to see hormones needed to take a back seat.

'Jeanie, this whole year is about being sensible. You're an attractive woman...'

She snorted.

'With a great smile and a big heart,' he continued. 'And if you put a single woman and a single man together for a year, then it's inevitable that sparks will fly. But we're both old enough and sensible enough to know how to douse those sparks.'

'So that's what we're doing for the next twelve months. Dousing sparks?' She ventured a smile. 'So do I pack the fire extinguisher today?'

'If we feel the smallest spark, we hit the water. The water temperature around here is barely above freezing. That should do it. Will you come?'

There was a moment's hesitation and then: 'Foolish or not, I never could resist a puffin,' she told him. 'My only stipulation is that you don't wear a kilt. Because sparks are all very well, Alasdair McBride, but you put a kilt on that body and sparks could well turn into a wildfire.'

He was free to make of that as he willed. She turned away, grabbed a picnic basket and started to pack.

He couldn't just manage a boat; he was one with the thing.

Jeanie had been in enough boats with enough men—she'd even worked as crew on Rory's fishing trawler—to recognise a seaman when she saw one.

Who could have guessed this smooth, suave businessman from Edinburgh, this kilted lord of all he surveyed at Duncairn, was a man who seemed almost as at home at sea as the fishermen who worked the island's waters.

The *Mary-Jane* was tied at the harbour wharf when they arrived, with a note from Dougal to Alasdair taped to the bollard.

Keep in radio contact and keep her safe. And I don't mean the boat.

Alasdair had grinned, leaped lightly onto the deck and turned to help Jeanie down. She'd ignored his hand and climbed down herself—a woman had some pride. And she was being very wary of sparks.

The *Mary-Jane* was a sturdy cabin cruiser, built to take emergency supplies out to a broken-down fishing trawler, or as a general harbour runabout. She was tough and serviceable—but so was the man at the helm. He was wearing faded trousers, heavy boots and an ancient sweater. He hadn't shaved this morning. He was looking…

Don't think about how he looks, she told herself fiercely, so instead she concentrated on watching him handle the boat. The Duncairn bar was tricky. You had to know your way, but Alasdair did, steering towards the right channel, then pausing, waiting, watching the sea on the far side, judging the perfect time to cross and then nailing it so they cruised across the bar as if they'd been crossing a lake.

And as they entered open water Jeanie found herself relaxing. How long since she'd done this? Taken a day just for her? Had someone think about her?

He wanted to see the puffins himself, she told herself, but a voice inside her head corrected her.

He didn't have to do this. He didn't have to bring me. He's doing it because I need a break.

It was a seductive thought all by itself.

And the day was seductive. The sun was warm on her face. Alasdair adjusted his course so they were facing into the waves, so she hardly felt the swell—but she did feel the power of the sea beneath them, and she watched Alasdair and she thought, There's power there, too.

He didn't talk. Maybe he thought she needed silence. She did and she was grateful. She sat and let the day, the sea, the sun soak into her.

This was as if something momentous had happened. This was as if she'd walked through a long, long tunnel and emerged to the other side.

Was it just because she'd taken the day off? Or was it that she'd set her future for the next twelve months, and for the next year she was safe?

It should be both, but she knew it wasn't. It was strange but sitting here in the sun, watching Alasdair, she had an almost overwhelming sense that she could let down her guard, lose the rigid control she'd held herself under since the appalling tragedy of Alan, let herself be just…Jeanie.

She'd lost who she was. Somewhere along the way she'd been subsumed. Jeffrey's daughter, Rory's girlfriend and wife, then Alan's woman.

Then bankrupt, with half the world seeming to be after her for money owed.

Then Eileen's housekeeper.

She loved being the housekeeper at Duncairn but the role had enveloped her. It was all she was.

But today she wasn't a housekeeper. She wasn't any of her former selves. Today she was out on the open sea, with a man at the helm who was…

Her husband?

There was nothing prescribed for her today except that she enjoy herself, and suddenly who could resist? She found herself smiling. Smiling and smiling.

'A joke?' Alasdair asked softly, and she turned her full beam onto him.

'No joke. I've just remembered why I love this place. I haven't been to sea for so long. And the puffins…I can't remember. How far out?'

'You mean, are we there yet?' He grinned back and it was a grin to make a girl open her eyes a little wider. It was a killer grin. 'Isn't that what every kid in the back seat asks?'

'That's what I feel like—a kid in the back seat.' And then she looked ahead to the granite rock needles that seemed to burst from the ocean floor, isolated in their grandeur. 'No, I don't,' she corrected herself. 'I feel like I'm a front-seat passenger. It's one of these rocks, isn't it, where the puffins are found?'

'The biggest one at the back. The smaller ones are simply rock but the back one has a landmass where they can burrow for nests. They won't nest anywhere humans can reach. It means we can't land.'

'We'd need a pretty long rope ladder,' Jeanie breathed, looking at the sheer rock face in awe. And then she forgot to breathe... 'Oh-h-h.'

It was a long note of discovery. It was a note of awe.

For Alasdair had manoeuvred the boat through a gap in the island rock face and emerged to a bay of calm water. The water was steel grey, fathoms deep, and it was a mass of...

Puffins. Puffins!

Alasdair cut the motor to just enough power to keep clear of the cliffs. The motor was muted to almost nothing.

The puffins were everywhere, dotted over the sea as if someone had sprinkled confetti—only this confetti was made up of birds, duck-sized but fatter, black and white with extraordinary bright orange bills; puffins that looked exactly like the ones Jeanie had seen in so many magazines, on so many posters, but only ever once in real life and that so long ago it seemed like a dream.

Comical, cute—beautiful.

'They have fish,' she breathed. 'That one has... It must be at least three fish. More. Oh, my...I'd forgotten. There's another. And another. Why don't they just swallow them all at once?'

'Savouring the pleasure?' Alasdair said, smiling just as Aladdin's genie might have done in the ancient fairy tale. Granting what he knew was a wish...

'You look like a benevolent Santa,' Jeanie told him and he raised his brows.

'Is that an accusation?'

'I... No.' Because it wasn't. It was just a statement.

Though he didn't actually look like Santa, Jeanie conceded. This was no fat, jolly old man.

Though she didn't need to be told that. His skill at the wheel was self-evident.

Sex on legs...

The description hit her with a jolt, and with it came a shaft of pure fear. Because that had been how she'd once thought of Alan.

Life with Rory had been...safe. He'd lived and

dreamed fishing and would never have left the island. He was content to do things as his father and grandfather had done before him. His mother cooked and cleaned and was seemingly content, so he didn't see that Jeanie could possibly want more.

He was a good man, solid and dependable, and his death had left Jeanie devastated. But two years later Alan had blasted himself into her life. She'd met him and she'd thought…

Yep, sex on legs.

More. She'd thought he was everything Rory hadn't been. He was exciting, adventurous, willing and wanting to try everything life had to offer. He'd taken her off the island and exposed her to a life that…

That she never wanted to go back to. A life that was shallow, mercenary, dangerous—even cruel.

Alan was a McBride, just as this man was.

Sex on legs? Get a grip, she told herself. Have you learned nothing? The only one who'll keep yourself safe is yourself.

But she didn't *want* to be safe, a little voice whispered, and she looked at Alasdair and she could see the little voice's reasoning but she wasn't going there. She wasn't.

'If you want to know the truth, I read about them last night,' Alasdair told her. He was watching the puffins—thankfully. How much emotion could he read in her face? 'They can carry up to ten small fish in their beaks at a time. It's a huge genetic advantage—they don't waste energy swallowing and regurgitating, and they can carry up to ten fish back to their burrows. Did you know their burrows can be up to two feet deep? And those beaks are only bright orange in the breeding season. They'll shed the colour soon and go back to being drab and ordinary.'

'They could never be ordinary,' she managed, turning to watch a puffin floating by the boat with…how many fish in its beak? Five. She got five.

She was concentrating fiercely on counting. Alasdair was still talking…and he usually didn't talk. He'd swotted up for today, she thought. Was finding out how many fish a puffin could hold a seduction technique?

The thought made her smile. No, she decided, and it settled her. He was taking her out today simply to be nice. He wasn't interested in her, or, if he was, it'd be a mere momentary fancy, as Alan's had been.

So get yourself back to basics, she told herself. Eileen had offered Alan money to marry her. She knew that now. The knowledge had made her feel sick, and here was another man who'd been paid to marry her.

Sex on legs? Not so much. He was a husband who was hers because of money.

Hold that thought.

'Will we eat lunch here?' she asked, suddenly brisk, unwinding herself from the back seat on the boat and heading for the picnic basket. 'Can you throw down anchor or should we eat on the way back?'

'We have time to eat here.' He was watching her, his brows a question. 'Jeanie, how badly did Alan hurt you?'

'I have sandwiches and quiche and salad and boiled eggs. I also have brownies and apples. There's beer, wine or soda. Take your pick.'

'You mean you're not going to tell me?'

'Past history. Moving on…'

'I won't hurt you.'

'I know you won't,' she said briskly. 'Because I won't let you. This is a business arrangement, Alasdair, nothing more.'

'And today?'

'Is my payment for past services.' She was finding it hard to keep her voice even but she was trying. 'You've offered and I've accepted. It's wonderful—no, it's magic—to be eating lunch among the puffins. It's a gift. I'm very, very grateful but I'm grateful as an employee's grateful to her boss for a day off. Nothing more.'

'It's not a day off. It's a week almost completely off and then I'm halving your duties for double the wages.'

Whoa? Double wages?

She should refuse, she thought, but then…why not just be a grateful employee? That was what she was, after all.

'Excellent,' she said and passed the sandwiches. 'Take a sandwich—sir.'

Employer/employee. That was a relationship that'd work, he thought, and it was fine with him—wasn't it?

He was grateful to Jeanie. She'd agreed to marry him, and in doing so she'd saved the estate. More, she'd made Eileen's last years happy. He was doing what he could to show he was grateful and she was accepting with pleasure.

It should be enough.

Their puffin expedition was magic. For Alasdair, who'd seen them so often in the past, they should feel almost commonplace, but in watching Jeanie watch them he was seeing them afresh. They were amazing creatures—and Jeanie's reaction was magic.

She tried hard to be prosaic, he thought. Her reactions to him were down-to-earth and practical, and she tried to tone down her reactions to the birds, but he watched her face, he watched the awe as she saw the birds dive and come up with beaks stuffed with rows of silver fish, he watched her turn her face to the sun and he thought, Here was a woman who'd missed out on the joy of life until now.

It was a joy to be able to share.

They returned to the castle late afternoon to find all the tasks done, the castle spotless, the grass mowed, the cattle tended. Jeanie entered the amazing great hall and looked up at the newly washed leadlight, the carpets beaten, the great oak balustrades polished, and he thought he detected the glimmer of tears.

But she said nothing, just gave a brisk nod and headed for her kitchen.

The baking was done. A Victoria sponge filled with strawberries and cream and a basket of chocolate brownies were sitting on the bench. Jeanie stared at them blankly.

'What am I going to do now?' she demanded.

'Eat them,' Alasdair said promptly. 'Where's a knife?'

'Don't you dare cut the sponge. The guests can have it for supper. You can have what's left.'

'Aren't I a guest?'

'Okay, you can have some for supper,' she conceded. 'But not first slice.'

'Because?'

'Because you're the man in the middle. Guest without privileges.'

'Guest with brownie,' he retorted and bit into a still-warm cookie. 'So tomorrow...otters?'

'What do you mean, otters?'

'I mean Maggie's mam and her friends are hired to come every weekday until I tell them not, and I haven't seen the Duncairn otters for years. They used to live in the burns running into the bay. I thought we could take a picnic down there and see if we can see them. Meanwhile I'm off to work now, Jeanie. You can go put your feet up, read a book, do whatever you want, whatever you haven't been able to do for the last few years. I'll see you at dinner.'

'Guests eat out,' she said blankly, but he shook his head.

'Sorry, Jeanie, but as you said, I'm the man in the middle. I'm a guest, but I'm also Lord of this castle. I'm also, for better or for worse, your husband.'

'There was nothing in the marriage contract about me feeding you.'

'That's why I'm feeding you,' he told her and at the look on her face he grinned. 'And no, I'm not about to whisk you off to a Michelin-ranked restaurant, even if such a thing existed on Duncairn, but Maggie's mam has brought me the ingredients for a very good risotto and risotto is one of the few things in the world I'm good at. So tonight I'm cooking.'

'I don't want—'

'There are lots of things we don't want,' he said, gentling now. 'This situation is absurd but there's nothing for it but for us both to make the most of it. Risotto or nothing, Jeanie.'

She stared at him for a long moment and then, finally, she gave a brisk nod. 'Fine,' she said. 'Good. I...I'll eat your risotto and thank you for it. And thank you for today. Now I'll…I'll…go do a stocktake of…of the whisky. There's all the new stuff you've bought. I keep a ledger. Call me when dinner's ready…sir…'

'Alasdair,' he snapped.

'Alasdair,' she conceded. 'Call me when dinner's ready. And thank you.'

She fled and he stood staring after her.

She was accepting his help. It should be enough.

Only it wasn't.

She felt weird. Discombobulated. Thoroughly disoriented. For the first time in over three years she had nothing to do.

Except think of the day that had just been.

Except think of Alasdair?

He was her husband. She should be used to having husbands by now. He was nothing different.

Except he was. He'd spent today working for nothing except her enjoyment.

He'd seen puffins many times before—the way he looked at them told her that. He also had work to do. She'd heard him at the computer almost all the time he'd been here. She'd heard the insistent ring of his telephone. Alasdair McBride was the head of a gigantic web of financial enterprises, and one look at the Internet had told her just how powerful that web was.

He'd spent the day making her happy.

'Because I agreed to keep our bargain,' she told herself. 'I'm saving his butt.

'The best way for him to keep his butt safe is for him to keep a low profile.' The dogs, well-fed and exercised, were sprawled in front of the kitchen range. They were fast asleep but she needed someone—anyone—to talk to. 'He must know that, and yet he risked it…

'To make me happy?' She thought of Rory doing such a thing. Rory was always too tired, she conceded. He had long spells at sea and when he was home he wanted his armchair and the telly. He'd taken time to spend with her before they were married but afterwards…it was as if he no longer had to bother.

And Alan? That was the same thing multiplied by a million. Pounds. He'd had well over a million reasons to marry her but when he had what he wanted, she was nothing.

And Alasdair? He, too, had more than a million reasons to marry her, she thought, way more, but she'd agreed to his deal. He'd had no reason to spend today with her.

'Maybe he thinks I'll back out,' she told the dogs but she knew it wasn't that.

Or maybe it was that she hoped it wasn't that.

'And that's just your stupid romantic streak,' she told herself crossly. 'And, Jeanie Lochlan, it's more than time you were over that nonsense.'

Her discussion with herself was interrupted by her phone. Maggie, she thought, and sure enough her friend was on the line, and Maggie was almost bursting with curiosity.

'How did it go? Oh, Jeanie, isn't he gorgeous? I watched you go out through the entrance with the field glasses—I imagine half the village did. Six hours you were out. Six hours by yourself with the man! And the amount he's given Dougal for the *Mary-Jane*, and what he's paying Mam and her friends… Jeanie, what are you doing not being in bed with your husband right now?'

She took a deep breath at that. 'He's not my real husband,' she managed but Maggie snorted.

'You could have fooled me. And Mam says he was just lovely on the phone and he's thanked her for the sponge cake and the brownies as though she wasn't even paid for them, and he's organised her to go back tomorrow and he says he's taking you to see otters. Otters! You know the old cottage down by the Craigie Burn? There's otters down there, I'm sure of it. You could light a fire and—'

'Maggie!'

'It's just a suggestion. Jeanie, you married the man and if you aren't in bed with him already you should be. Oh, Jeanie, I know he's not like Alan, I know it.'

'You've hardly met him.'

'The way he said his vows…'

'We were both lying and you know it.'

'I don't know it,' Maggie said stoutly. 'You went home last night, didn't you? One night married, three hundred and sixty-four to go—or should I multiply that by fifty years? Jeanie, do yourself a favour and go for it. Go for him.'

'Why would I?'

There was a moment's silence while Maggie collected her answer. One of the guest's cars was approaching. Jeanie could see it through the kitchen window. She took a plate and started arranging brownies. This was her job, she told herself. Her life.

'Because he can afford—' Maggie started but Jeanie cut her off before she could finish.

'He can afford anything he wants,' she conceded. 'But that's thanks to me. I told you how Eileen's will works. He gets to keep his fortune and I... I get to keep my independence. That's the way I want it, Maggie, and that's the way it's going to be.'

'But you will go to see the otters tomorrow?'

'Yes,' she said, sounding goaded. Which was how she felt, she conceded. She'd been backed into a corner, and she wasn't at all sure she could extricate herself.

By keeping busy, she told herself, taking the brownies off the plate and rearranging them more...artistically.

One day down, three hundred and sixty-four to go.

CHAPTER SEVEN

THEY DID GO to look for otters, and Alasdair decreed they would go to Craigie Burn. It was the best place to see otters, he told her, the furthest place on the estate from any road, a section of the burn where otters had hunted and fished for generations almost undisturbed. The tiny burnside cottage had been built by a long-ago McBride who'd fancied fishing and camping overnight in relative comfort. But at dusk and dawn the midges appeared in their hordes and the fishing McBride of yore had soon decided that the trek back to the comforts of the castle at nightfall was worth the effort. The cottage had therefore long fallen into disrepair. The roof was intact but the place was pretty much a stone shell.

Jeanie hadn't intended telling Alasdair about Craigie Burn—but of course he knew.

'I spent much of my childhood on the estate,' he told her as they stowed lunch into the day pack. 'I had the roaming of the place.'

'Alan, too?' she asked because she couldn't help herself. Alan had hardly talked of his childhood—he'd hardly talked of his family.

'My father and Alan's father were peas in a pod,' he said curtly. 'They were interested in having a good time and not much else. They weren't interested in their sons. Both our childhoods were therefore lonely but Alan thought he was lonelier here. The few times Eileen brought him here he hated it.'

He swung the pack onto his back and then appeared to check Jeanie out—as she checked the guests out before they went rambling, making sure boots were stout, clothing sensible, the wildness of the country taken into account when dressing. He gave a curt nod. 'Good.' The dogs were locked in the wet room. Maggie's mam would see them walked, for if the dogs were with them the possibility of seeing otters was about zero. 'Ready?'

'Ready,' she said, feeling anything but. What was she doing traipsing around the country with this man when she should be earning her keep?

But Alasdair was determined to give her a… honeymoon? Whatever it was called, it seemed she had no choice but to give in to him. She was still getting over sitting at the kitchen table the night before eating the risotto he'd prepared. It was excellent risotto, but...

But the man had her totally off balance.

They set off, down the cliff path to the rocky beach, then along the seafront, clambering over rocks, making their way to where Craigie Burn tumbled to the sea.

The going was tough, even for Jeanie, who was used to it. Alasdair, though, had no trouble. A few times he paused and turned to help her. She shook off his offer of assistance but in truth his concern made her feel...

As she had no right to feel, she told herself. She didn't need to feel like the 'little woman'. She'd had two marriages of being a doormat. No more.

'Tell me about your childhood here,' she encouraged as she struggled up one particularly rocky stretch. She asked more to take Alasdair's attention away from her heavy breathing than out of interest—she would not admit she was struggling.

But instead of talking as he climbed, Alasdair turned and gazed out to sea. Did he sense how much she needed a breather? He'd better not, she thought. I will not admit I'm a lesser climber than he is.

But…without admitting anything…she turned and gazed out to sea with him.

'I loved it,' he said at last, and it had taken so long to answer she'd almost forgotten she'd asked. But his gaze was roving along the coastline, rugged, wild, amazing. 'My father and my uncle hardly spent any time here. They hated it. My grandparents sent them to boarding school in England and they hardly came back. They both married socialites, they lived in the fast lane on my grandparents' money and they weren't the least bit interested in their sons. But Alan loved their lifestyle—from the time he was small he wanted to be a part of it. He loved the fancy hotels, the servants, the parties. It was only me who hated it.'

'So you came back here.'

'We were dumped,' he told her. 'Both of us. Our parents dumped us with Eileen every school holidays and she thought the castle would be good for us. Alan chafed to be able to join his parents' lifestyle.' He gave a wry smile. 'Maybe I was just antisocial even then, but here…'

He paused and looked around him again. A pair

of eagles was soaring in the thermals. She should be used to them by now, she told herself, but every time she saw them she felt her heart swell. They were magnificent and Alasdair paused long enough for her to know he felt it, too.

'Here was home,' Alasdair said at last. 'Here I could be myself. Eileen usually stayed when Alan and I were here. You saw the place before she renovated. She and my grandfather didn't appear to notice conditions were a bit…sparse. I don't think I noticed, either. I was too busy, exploring, fishing, trying not to think how many days I had left before I went back to school. Alan was counting off the days until he could leave. I wanted to stay for the rest of my life.'

'You didn't, though. You ended up based in Edinburgh. You hardly came here until…until Eileen got sick at the end.'

She was trying hard not to make her words an accusation but she didn't get it right. It sounded harsh.

There was a long silence. 'I didn't mean to be accusatory,' she ventured at last and he shook his head.

'I know you didn't. But I need to explain. At first I didn't come because I was immersed in business. I took to the world of finance like a duck to water, and maybe I lost perspective on other things I loved. But then… When Eileen started spending more time here, I didn't come because you were here.'

That was enough to give a girl pause. To make her forget to breathe for a moment. 'Did you dislike me so much?' she asked in a small voice and he gave an angry shrug.

'I didn't know you, but I knew Alan. I knew I hated him.'

'Because?'

'Because he was the sort of kid who pulled wings off flies. I won't sugar coat it. My father was older than his, so my father stood to inherit the title, with me coming after him. Alan's father resented mine and the resentment was passed on down the line. I don't know what sort of poison was instilled in Alan when he was small but he was taught to hate me and he knew how to hurt.'

Whoa. He hadn't talked of this before. She knew it instinctively and who knew how she knew it, but she did. What he was saying was being said to her alone—and it hurt to say it.

His eyes went to a point further along the coast, where the burn met the sea. 'It came to a head down here,' he told her, absently, almost as if speaking to the land rather than her. Apologising for not being back for so long? 'I loved the otters, and I used to come down here often. One day Alan followed me. I was lying on my stomach watching the otters through field glasses. He was up on the ridge, and he'd taken my grandfather's shotgun. He killed three otters before I reached him. He was eighteen months older than me, and much bigger, and I went for him and he hit me with the gun. I still carry the scar under my hairline. I was dazed and bleeding, and he laughed and walked back to the castle.'

'No…'

His mouth set in a grim line. 'Thinking back… that blow to my head… He nearly killed me. But I was twelve and he was fourteen, and I was afraid of him. I told Grandmother I'd fallen on the cliffs. Soon after that his parents decided he was old enough to join them in the resorts they stayed at, so I didn't have to put up with him any more. I never told Eileen what happened. In retrospect, maybe I should have.' And then he paused and looked at her. 'But you… You loved him?'

'No.'

'It doesn't matter. It's none of my business, but

these last years… Just knowing you were here in the castle was enough to keep me away.'

'I'm so sorry.'

'You shouldn't have to apologise for your husband's faults.'

'But as you said, I married him.'

'I can't see you killing otters.'

'Is that why you took me to look at the puffins first?' she asked. 'To see how I reacted?'

'I was hardly expecting a gun.'

'I'd guess you weren't expecting a gun from Alan, either.' She sighed and took a deep breath— and it wasn't only because she needed a few deep breaths before tackling the rise in front of her. 'Okay, I understand. Alasdair, we don't need to go there any more. I'll stop judging you for not spending more time with your grandmother if you stop judging me for being married to Alan. I know I'm still…tainted…but we can work around that. Deal?'

He looked at her for a long moment, seeming to take in every inch of her. And then, slowly, his face creased into a smile.

It was an awesome smile, Jeanie thought. It was dark turning to light. It lit his whole face, made his dark eyes glint with laughter, made him seem softer, more vulnerable…

A warrior exposed?

That shouldn't be how she saw him, but suddenly it was. He was the Earl of Duncairn, and he wore armour, just as surely as his ancestors wore chain mail. His armour might be invisible but it was still there.

Telling her about the otters, telling her about Alan, had made a chink in that armour, she thought, and even though he was smiling she could see the hint of uncertainty. As if telling her had left him vulnerable and he didn't like it.

She had a sudden vision of him as a child, here in this castle. It was wild now; it would have been wilder then. Eileen had told her she'd brought both boys here during their school holidays. Jeanie had envisaged two boys with a whole estate to explore and love.

But later Eileen had said she'd often had to leave the boys with the housekeeper when she'd had to go back to Edinburgh, and Jeanie saw that clearly now, too. A twelve-year-old boy would have been subjected to the whims and cruelty of his older cousin. It wouldn't just have been the otters, she thought grimly. She knew Alan.

There would have been countless cruelties during the years.

'This next bit's rough,' Alasdair was saying and he held his hand out. 'Let me help you.'

She looked down at his hand.

He was a McBride. He was yet another man who'd caught her at a weak moment and married her.

But the day was magic, the hill in front was tough and Alasdair was right beside her, smiling, holding out his hand.

'If I had one more brain cell, it'd be lonely,' she muttered out loud, to no one in particular, but Alasdair just raised his brows and kept on smiling and the sun was warm on her face and the otters were waiting, and a woman was only human after all.

She put her hand in his and she started forward again.

With Alasdair.

What followed was another magic day. Duncairn's weather was unpredictable to say the least, but today the gods had decided to be kind— more, they'd decided to put on Scotland at her most splendid. There was just enough wind to keep the midges at bay. The sky was dotted by clouds that might or might not turn to rain, but for now the sun shone, and the water in the burn was crystal clear.

Without hesitation Alasdair led them to a ledge near the cottage, a rocky outcrop covered with a thick layer of moss. It stretched out over the burn, but a mere ten feet above, so they could lie on their stomachs and peer over the edge to see what was happening in the water below.

And for a while nothing happened. Maybe it wouldn't, Alasdair conceded. Otters were notoriously shy. They could well have sensed their movement and darted back under cover, but for now they were content to wait.

Alasdair was more than content.

It was a strange feeling, lying on the moss-covered rock with Jeanie stretched out by his side.

His life was city-based now, mostly spent in Edinburgh but sometimes London, New York, Copenhagen, wherever the demands of his company took him. Under the terms of Eileen's will he'd need to delegate much of that travel for the next year. He'd thought he'd miss it, but lying next to Jeanie, waiting for otters to grace them with their presence, he thought suddenly, *Maybe I won't*.

What other woman had he ever met who'd lie on her stomach on a rock and not move, not say a word, and somehow exude a quality of complete restfulness? After half an hour the otters still hadn't shown themselves. He knew from past experience that half an hour wasn't long for these shy creatures to stay hidden, but did Jeanie know that? If she did, she didn't mind. She lay with her chin resting on her hands, watching the water below, but her eyes were half-closed, almost contemplative.

Her hair was tumbling down around her face. A curl was blocking his view. He wanted to lift it away.

She'd been Alan's wife.

Surely it didn't matter. He wanted to touch...

But if he moved he'd scare the otters, and he knew...he just knew that this woman would be furious with him—not just for touching her but for spoiling what she was waiting for.

She was waiting for otters, not for him.

Right. Watch on. He managed to turn his attention back to the water rippling beneath them.

'There...' It was hardly a whisper. Jeanie was

looking left to where a lower overhang shaded the water, and there it was, a sleek, beautiful otter slipping from the shadows, with a younger one behind.

'Oh,' Jeanie breathed. 'Oh…'

She was completely unaware of him. All her attention was on the otters.

They were worth watching. They were right out from under the shadows now, slipping over the burn's rocky bed, nosing through the sea grasses and kelp, hunting for the tiny sea creatures that lived there.

'They eat the kelp, too,' Jeanie whispered but Alasdair thought she was talking to herself, not to him.

'They're stunning,' he whispered back. 'Did you know their coat's so thick not a single drop of water touches their skin?'

'That's why they're hunted,' she whispered back. 'You will…keep protecting them? After I've left?'

And there it was again—reality, rearing its ugly head. At the end of this year, this castle would go to Jeanie's creditors. He'd buy it and keep it—of course he would. He'd keep it safe. But he glanced at Jeanie and saw her expression and he thought, She's not sure.

He'd promised—but this woman must have been given empty promises in the past.

She was resting her chin on her hands and he could see the gold band he'd placed on her finger two days ago. For a year they were required to be officially married, and officially married people wore rings.

But now… What worth was a promise? Jeanie didn't trust him and why should she?

He glanced down at the otters, hunting now in earnest, despite the humans close by. They must sense their shadows, but they'd waited for almost an hour before resuming hunting. They'd be hungry. They'd be forced to trust.

As Jeanie had been forced to trust. She'd been put into an impossible situation. How to tell her…?

The ring…

One moment she was lying watching otters, worrying about their future, thinking would Alasdair really keep this estate? Would he keep caring for these wild creatures she'd come to love?

The next moment he'd rolled back a little

and was tugging at his hand. Not his left hand, though, where she'd placed the wedding ring that meant so little. Instead he was tugging at his right hand.

At the Duncairn ring.

She'd seen this ring. It was in every one of the portraits of the McBride earls, going back in time until the names blurred and Eileen's history lesson had started seeming little more than a roll call.

Each of those long-dead earls had worn this ring, and now it lay on Alasdair's hand. It was a heavy gold signet, an intricate weaving, the head of an eagle embossed on a shield, with the first letters of the family crest, worn but still decipherable, under the eagle's beak: LHV.

Loyalty, honour, valour.

Alan had mentioned this ring, not once, but often. 'He's a prig,' he'd said of Alasdair. 'And he's younger than me. He thinks he can lord it over me just because he wears the damned ring...'

The 'damned ring' was being held out to her. No, not held out. Alasdair was taking her hand in his and sliding the ring onto the middle finger of her right hand. It fitted—as if it was meant to be there.

She stared down at it, stunned. So much history in one piece of jewellery... So many McBride men who'd worn this ring...

'Wh-what do you think you're doing?' she stammered at last, because this didn't make sense.

'Pledging my troth.'

'Huh?' Dumb, she thought, but that was how she was feeling. Dumb. And then she thought: she shouldn't be here. Her fragile control felt like crumbling. This man seemed as large and fierce and dangerous as the warriors he'd descended from.

Loyalty, honour, valour...

This was the McBride chieftain. He was placing a ring on her finger, and the ring took her breath away.

'Jeanie, I have nothing else to show you I'm serious.' In the kirk, Alasdair's vows had been businesslike, serious, but almost...clinical. Here, now, his words sounded as if they came from the heart. 'I'm promising you that at the end of this year of marriage I will make your life secure. As well, I will buy this castle for what it's worth and

Alan's creditors will be paid. I'll treat it as the last of Alan's share of the estate. He was, after all, just as much Eileen's grandson as I was.'

'You don't have to make me secure,' she managed, still staring at the ring. 'And Alan wasn't worth—'

'I'm not judging,' he told her. 'And I refuse to think of Alan after this. To be honest, it took courage to come here. I haven't been back to this place since that day he hurt the otters. But I have come, to find life has moved on. But it needs faith to face it. So here's my faith in you, and I'm hoping you can find that faith in me. At the end of the year I'll take on this estate and I'll care for it as Eileen would have wanted it cared for. And as I suspect you want it cared for. And I will ensure your future...'

'I don't want anything.'

'I know you don't. You don't seem to put yourself into the equation at all, but I'm putting you there. It seems you canna keep the castle, Jeanie lass, no matter what Eileen's will says, but you can keep the heart of it. As long as you wear this ring, this estate will be safe, our Jeanie. I promise you. Hand on this ring, I swear.'

He'd lapsed into broad Scottish, the voice of

his ancestors, the voice of his people. He was lying full-length on a bed of moss over a rippling burn, he was looking at her as no man had ever looked at her, and the way he spoke… It was as if he were kneeling before a throne, head bowed, swearing fealty to his king.

Swearing fealty to…her?

'Alasdair…' It was hard to breathe, much less speak. She had to fight for the words. 'There's no need,' she managed. 'You don't have to do this. Besides…' She stared at the intricate weaving of gold on her finger and her heart failed her. 'I'll probably lose it in a pudding mix.'

He smiled then, but his smile was perfunctory, the gravity of the moment unchanged. 'I know you won't. I trust you with it, Jeanie, as you trust me with the castle.' His hand closed over hers, folding her fingers, the ring enclosed between them. 'I'm asking that you trust me back.'

'I can… I can trust you without the ring.'

'Why would you?'

'Because…' How to say it? There were no words.

And the truth was that until now, until this moment, she hadn't trusted. Yes, he was Lord of Duncairn but he was just another man, like her father, like Rory, like Alan. A man to be wary of. A man who sought to control.

Was this ring another form of control? She searched for the control angle, and couldn't find it.

She had no doubt as to the significance of this ring. She could hear it in his voice—that it meant as much to him as it had to every other earl who'd ever worn it.

Trust… He was offering it in spades.

'I'll give it back,' she managed. 'At the end of the year.'

'You'll give it to me when you've seen what I intend doing with this place,' he told her. 'When you see me hand the wilderness areas over to a trust to keep it safe in perpetuity. When you have total faith, Jeanie McBride, then you can give it back.'

'I have faith now.'

'You don't,' he said softly and his hold on her hand tightened. 'You can't. But you will.'

And then it rained.

She'd been so caught up, first with the otters and then with…well, with what she'd been caught up with, that she hadn't noticed the clouds scudding in from the west. Now, suddenly, the sun disappeared and the first fat droplets splashed down.

And Alasdair was tugging her to her feet, smiling, as if something had been settled between them that made going forward easy.

Maybe it had.

And maybe, Jeanie thought as she scrambled with Alasdair to reach the shelter of the cottage, as she didn't quibble about the feel of his hand still holding hers, as she fought to regain her breath and composure, maybe something had settled inside her as well.

Trust? She'd never trusted. She'd walked into this marriage blind, knowing only that circumstances once again had thrust her into making vows. But now… For some reason it was as if a weight was lifting from her shoulders, a weight she hadn't known she was carrying.

This year could work. This year could almost be…fun? Such a word was almost nonexistent in her vocabulary. As a child of a dour, grim fisherman and then as Rory's wife, a man under the thumb of his family, a man with limited horizons and no ambition to change, life had been hard and pretty much joyless. Life with Alan, so tantalising at first, had ended up filled with nothing but terror, and since that time she'd been subsumed with guilt, with debt, with responsibilities.

Today, though…today she'd lain in the sun and watched otters and this man had given her his ancestral ring. He'd given her trust…

And then he pushed open the cottage door and all thoughts of trust went out of the window.

She'd been in this cottage before. She'd walked this way with the dogs—it was a fair trek from the castle but at times during the past three years she'd needed the effort it required. Sometimes trekking the estate was the only way to get rid of the demons in her head, but even when she was fighting demons she still liked staying dry. On the west coast of Scotland rain came sudden and fierce. She'd walked and watched the sky— as they hadn't today—and she'd used this cottage for shelter.

She knew it. Any furniture had long gone, the windows were open to the elements and the place seemed little more than a cave.

But today… Someone had been in here before them. The room they walked into was a combination of kitchen/living, with a hearth at one end. The hearth had always been blackened and empty, but now... It contained a massive heap of glowing coals. Firewood was stacked beside it. The stone floor in front of it had been swept of debris and a rug laid in front. With the fire at its heart, the room looked almost cosy.

She hadn't noticed smoke from the chimney. Why?

She'd been too aware of Alasdair, that was why. Of all the stupid...

'How on earth...?' she managed, staring at the fire in disbelief, and Alasdair looked smug.

'Insurance,' he told her. 'There's never a day on this island when you're guaranteed of staying dry, and I'm a cautious man. I never take risks without insurance.' But he was frowning at the rug. 'I didn't ask for the rug, though. That's a bit over the top.'

'You think?' Her voice was practically a squeak. 'Who did this? Not you. Surely...'

'You don't think I could have loped up here before breakfast?'

'No!' And her tone was so adamant that he grinned.

'That's not a very complimentary way to talk to your liege lord.'

She told him where he could put his liege lord

and his grin widened. 'I talked to Mac about getting the fire lit,' he confessed. 'Mac can't walk up here himself any more—I need to do something about gillie succession planning—but he does know a lad, who came up here and lit it for him.'

'A lad?' Jeanie breathed. And then she closed her eyes. 'No.' It was practically a groan. 'It won't be one lad. It'll be two. He'll have asked Lachlan and Hamish McDonald, two of the biggest wastrels this island's ever known. They're twins, they're forty, their mother still irons their socks and they do odd jobs when they feel like it. And they gossip. Mac's their uncle. Do you realise what you've done? This'll be all over the island before we get back to the castle that you and I have lain by the fire here and…and…'

'And what, Jeanie?' His smile was still there but his eyes had become…watchful?

'And nothing,' she snapped and walked forward and grabbed the backpack from his shoulders and started to unpack. 'We'll eat the sandwiches I made and then we'll go home. And why did you pack wine? If you think I could climb these crags after a drink…'

'I could carry you.' He sounded almost hopeful.

'You and whose bulldozer? Get real.' She was totally flustered, trying to haul the lunch box from the backpack, trying not to look at him. She tugged it free with a wrench and shoved it down onto the hearth.

Alasdair stooped. His hand came over hers before she could rise again and his laughter died.

'I'm not into seduction,' he told her. His words echoed into the stillness. 'You're safe, Jeanie. This fire's here to keep us warm and dry, nothing more. I won't touch you.'

There was a long pause. 'I never said you'd try,' she said at last.

'You look like you expect it.'

She was struggling, trying to get it right, trying to explain this…panic. 'It's this ring,' she said at last. She stared down at the magnificent Duncairn signet and she felt…small. Frightened? At the edge of a precipice?

But still Alasdair's hand was over hers, warm, steady, strong. They were crouched before the fire. His face in the firelight was strong and sure.

'The ring is simply a promise,' he told her. 'It's a promise to keep the faith, to keep your faith. You needn't fear. I'm not into taking women against their will.'

'Not even...' Her voice was scarcely a whisper. 'Not even the woman you've taken as your wife?'

'You're not my wife,' he said, evenly now. 'We both know that this is a business relationship, despite what Hamish and Lachie may well have told the islanders. So let's have our sandwiches, and I intend to drink at least one glass of this truly excellent wine—my grandmother kept a superb cellar. You can join me or not, but whatever you do, my Jeanie, know that seduction is off the agenda.'

Which was all very well, she thought crossly as she did what was sensible. She ate her sandwiches and she drank one glass—only one—of wine, and she thought she should have settled, but why did he have to have called her *my Jeanie*? And *Jeanie lass*?

It was merely familiar, she told herself as she cleared their debris into the backpack. Any number of the older folk on the island called her Jeanie lass. Any number of islanders referred to her as our Jeanie.

But Alasdair McBride was not a member of the island's older folk. Nor was he really an islander.

It shouldn't matter. It didn't matter.

It did. It made her feel…

Scared.

'It does seem a shame to waste the rug. Do you want a nap before we head back?' Alasdair was watching her—and the low-life was laughing again. But not laughing out loud. It was more a glint behind his eyes, a telltale quiver of the corners of his mouth, the way his eyes met hers…

Laughter never seemed too far away. What did this man have to laugh about? she demanded of herself. Didn't he know life was hard?

But it wasn't hard for him. This man was the Earl of Duncairn. He could laugh at what he wanted.

He could laugh at her if he wanted. She couldn't afford to respond.

'It's stopped raining and we're getting out of here fast,' she said with acerbity. 'I wouldn't be surprised if there are field glasses trained on this doorway right now. There's no way I'm having the islanders conjecturing about my supposed love life.'

'They're conjecturing already,' he told her. 'And there's hardly shame attached. We are married.'

'We're not married,' she snapped again. 'Do

you want to see the otters again before we head back?'

'Yes.' The sun was shining again. 'Why not?'

'Then let's go,' she told him. 'But keep twenty paces distant, Alasdair McBride, and no closer or this ring gets tossed in the burn.'

'You wouldn't.' She'd touched him on the raw then; his face had even paled. She relented. Some things were too precious to even joke about.

'No. I wouldn't. Are you sure you don't want it back?'

'I don't want it back,' he told her. 'I trust you. And you can trust me, Jeanie, whether it's at twenty paces or a whole lot closer.'

A whole lot closer? There was the crux of the matter, she decided. He was too gorgeous for his own good.

Her problem was, she thought as she lay in bed that night and stared up into the darkness…her major problem was that she wouldn't mind getting a whole lot closer to Alasdair.

Or just a bit?

No. At three in the morning her mind was crystal clear and there was no way she could escape honesty. A whole lot closer was what she wanted.

She was out of her mind. A whole lot closer was exactly what sensible Jeanie would never allow herself to think about.

Except she was thinking about it. She was lying sleepless in the small hours. Alasdair's wedding band lay on one finger, his ancestral signet lay on another and she felt...she felt...

'Like a stupid serving maid having ideas above my station,' she told herself crossly and threw back the covers and went to stare out of the window.

She could see the sea from her bedroom. The moon was almost full, sending streams of silver across the water, almost into her room. It felt as if she could walk out of the bedroom and keep on walking...

'As maybe you should if you feel like this,' she told herself. 'Use some brains.

'I don't want to.'

Above her, in the vast, imposing bedroom that had been the bedroom of Earls of Duncairn for centuries past, lay the current Earl of Duncairn. The four-poster bed was enormous. His bedroom was enormous. Eileen had giggled when she'd been making decisions about restoring the castle and she'd told Jeanie she wanted a bedroom fit for a lord. Together they'd chosen rich velvet drapes, tapestries, rugs, furnishings…

To say it was lavish was an understatement. Apart from the servants' rooms she used and had—with some difficulty—kept free from Eileen's sumptuous plans, this castle was truly astonishing.

'It's enough to make its lord feel he can snap his fingers and any servant girl will come running,' she said out loud and then she caught her breath with where her thoughts were taking her.

This servant girl wouldn't mind running—but this servant girl should turn and run as far from this castle as possible.

'I was good today,' she told herself. 'I was sensible.

'Excellent,' she told herself. 'That's two days down, three hundred and sixty-three to go.'

But… There was a voice whispering in the back of her head and it wasn't a small voice, either. You're married to him. It wouldn't hurt.

'Are you out of your mind? Of course it'll hurt.' She ran her fingers through her tangled curls and the signet ring caught and hurt. 'Excellent,' she told herself. 'Just keep doing that. Pull your hair whenever you think of being an idiot.

'And he doesn't want you, anyway.'

She let her mind drift back to her mind-set when she'd married Rory. She'd still been a kid when she'd married him. He'd been safe, he'd been kind, and when she'd taken her vows she'd felt...as if a new net had been closing over her? He'd protected her from her father, and she'd been grateful, but that hadn't stopped her lying in bed at night after a wild night watching the telly feeling...was this all there was?

Which was why, two years after Rory's death, she'd been ripe for the picking. She had no doubt now that the only reason Alan had been attracted to her was to persuade his grandmother to give him money, but the means he'd used to attract... Excitement, adventure, travel had seemed a wild elixir, a drug impossible to resist, and by the time she'd woken to reality she'd been in so far it had been impossible to extricate herself.

And now here she was, wanting to...wanting to...

'I want nothing,' she told herself. 'For heaven's sake, Jeanie, grow a little sense. Put your head in a bucket of cold water if you must, but do not walk headlong into another emotional mess.'

* * *

'Get some sense.' On the floor above, in a bedroom so vast it made him feel ridiculous, Alasdair was staring at the slivers of moonlight lighting the dark and he was feeling pretty much the same.

'If you sleep with her, how the hell are you going to extricate yourself? You'll be properly married.

'There's no thought of sleeping with her.'

But there was. No matter how much his head told him it was crazy, his body was telling him something else entirely.

'It's just this stupid honeymoon idea,' he told himself. 'I never should have instigated it. Leave her to get back to her work and you get back to yours.'

Except…how long since she'd had a holiday? Yesterday and today she'd lit up. Clambering up the scree today, lying on the moss-covered rocks, watching the otters, she'd seemed younger, happier…free.

What had two husbands done to her? What had they done *for* her?

Saddled her with debt and regrets, that was what. Hell, she deserved a break.

'But not with me.' He said it out loud.

He should call off this honeymoon idea. But no, he couldn't do that. He'd told her they'd have a week.

She could have a week, he thought. She could do whatever she wanted, just not with him.

That's not a honeymoon.

'Right.' He was talking into the dark. 'It's not and it's not supposed to be.

'You'll tell her how?

'Straight out. She'll be relieved.

And what was there in that that made his gut twist?

Honesty. He could at least give her that. She deserved no less.

She deserved…

That he think seriously about what he was letting himself in for.

CHAPTER EIGHT

SHOULD ONE MAKE a special dinner to celebrate a one-month anniversary?

The weather had closed in, the sleet was driving from the north and she had no guests booked for the night. Jeanie was staring into the refrigerator, vacillating between sausages or something fancy. She had beef in the freezer. She had mushrooms for guests' breakfasts. She had excellent red wine, bought by Eileen and stocked in the castle larder.

Beef Bourguignon was hardly Scottish, but she could serve the rest of the red wine alongside, and make a lovely mash, and maybe make a good apple pie as well. She had clotted cream…

'And he'll eat it at his desk as he's eaten his dinner at his desk every night for the last month.' She slumped down at the table. The two dogs put their noses on her knee and whined.

'Yeah, the weather's getting to you, too,' she told them, but she knew it wasn't that. She'd grown up with Duncairn weather. She usually enjoyed the gales that blasted the island, donning wellies and mac and walking her legs off, the dogs at her side.

She'd walked her legs off this afternoon but it hadn't stopped the feeling of...desolation?

'Which is dumb,' she told the dogs and gave herself a mental shake. 'As is making any kind of anniversary dinner when all it means is that we've put up with each other for a month.

'And it's working okay,' she added after a moment, as if she was reassuring herself.

It was. Sort of. After the dumb idea of the honeymoon, which had lasted two days before he'd pulled out and she'd agreed with relief, Alasdair had decreed she have one day a week completely off. But not with him.

Their lives had settled into a pattern. She cared for the castle and the guests. Alasdair worked in his rooms or he headed to Edinburgh for the day. When that happened his chopper would arrive at dawn and bring him back before dusk, so one of his precious nights of freedom wouldn't be used up.

He walked but he walked alone. He kept himself to himself and she did the same.

He'd spent three nights in Hong Kong and it shouldn't have made any difference, but it did. The castle was empty for his going.

And now he was back. Today he was spending the entire day here. The weather was too rough for the chopper.

He was trapped—and that was how she felt, too. She worked on but she was so aware of him overhead. It was as if the entire month had been building. Every sense was tuned…

'And I'm getting stupid in my old age,' she told the dogs. 'I'm not a needy woman. I'm not.' She stared around the kitchen in frustration. She needed more to do. Anything. Fast.

Then the kitchen door swung open. Alasdair was standing there, in his casual trousers and sweater, his hair ruffled as if he'd raked it and raked it again.

'Jeanie?'

'Mmm?' Somehow she made herself sound non-committal. Somehow.

'This weather's driving me nuts.'

'You *are* on Duncairn.'

'I am,' he told her. 'And I'm thinking at the end of eleven months I'll be back in Edinburgh full-time and what will I have to show for these months? So I'm thinking… Jeanie, would you teach me to cook something other than spaghetti or risotto?'

If Duncairn had split in two and drifted in different directions in the sea, she couldn't have been more astonished.

'Cook,' she said blankly and he gave her a lop-sided smile.

'If you would.'

'Why?'

Why? The question hung in the air between them. It needed an answer and Alasdair was searching for one.

The fact that Jeanie was in the kitchen wasn't enough—though it was certainly a factor.

For the past month he'd put his head down and worked. Duncairn Enterprises took all his time and more. There seemed to be some sort of financial leak at head office. It was worrying, but over the past few weeks he'd almost welcomed it, sorting painstakingly through the remaining financial web his grandmother had controlled, rejecting the inclination to do anything else.

This afternoon he'd thought, Why? He could call in outside auditors to do what he'd been doing. He wasn't happy about letting outsiders look at possible financial problems of his grand-mother's making, but then his grandmother was past caring, and Jeanie was downstairs.

So why not go downstairs and join her? It had been an insistent niggle and this afternoon it had become a roar. Because he didn't want to get emotionally involved? He'd spent a month telling himself to form any sort of relationship would be courting catastrophe. If it didn't work out and she walked, it would be a disaster. He knew the way forward was to move with caution.

But for the past month he'd lived in the same house with Jeanie. He'd watched the dogs fly to meet her every time she left the house. He'd watched from his windows whenever she took them out, striding out across the pasture, stop-ping to speak to the cattle, the dogs wild with excitement at her side.

He'd listened to her sing as she did the house-work. He'd heard her laugh with the guests, or empathise with them about bad roads or lost suit-cases or general travel fatigue.

He'd eaten while he worked, separate from the other guests, working through a pile of papers a foot high, and he'd been aware of the aromas coming from the kitchen. He'd watched the dogs fly back and forth…

And this afternoon he'd cracked. He stood at the kitchen door and felt mildly foolish but hell, he was here, he'd said it and he was seeing this through.

And she'd asked why.

'I'm fed up with playing Lord of the castle,' he told her and she looked up at him and smiled.

'You can hardly knock back the title. It's what you are.'

'While you play servant.'

'That's what I am.'

'No.' It was an explosion that had the dogs starting out from under the table. Abbot even ventured a feeble bark.

'Your grandmother employed me to housekeep for the castle,' Jeanie said mildly. 'That's what I've been doing for the last three years. I have one more year to go.'

'You were Alan's wife. You deserve—'

'I deserve nothing for marrying Alan.'

'My grandmother thought you did.' Why was he getting into this conversation? He surely hadn't intended to.

'Your grandmother was kind and sentimental

and bossy. She felt sorry for me, end of story. Now if you'll excuse me, I need to get on...'

'Cooking. What do you intend to cook?'

'You're the only guest in the house tonight. What would you like me to cook?'

'I'm not a guest.'

'No, but in my mind that's how I'm seeing you. It keeps me sane. Now...requests? Sausages? Beef Bourguignon? Anything else that strikes your fancy?'

She was wearing a pink, frilly apron over her jeans and windcheater. It was tied with a big bow at the back, almost defiantly, as if she knew the bow was corny but she liked it anyway. She really was impossibly cute, he thought. Jeanie Lochlan, Domestic Goddess. Jeanie McBride...

His wife.

'Singing hinnies,' he told her. 'And I want to make them.'

'You're serious?'

'Do you know how to make them?' he asked.

'You're asking me, an islander born and bred, if I know how to make singing hinnies?'

'I'm sorry. Of course you do.'

'My granny's singing hinnies were famous.'

'Is the recipe a family secret?'

'Possibly.' She eyed him thoughtfully. 'Though some might say you're family now.'

And what was there in that to give him hope? He almost took the apron Jeanie took from the pantry and offered him. But it was pink, too. Did she expect him to wear a bow as well?

'You'll get batter on your lovely sweater.'

'I have more.'

'Of course you do,' she retorted and he looked at her—just looked.

'Oops,' she said and out peeped one of her gorgeous smiles. 'Servant giving master lip. Servant needs to learn to shut up.'

'Jeanie?'

'Yes...sir?'

'Teach me to cook,' he demanded and she saluted and her smile widened. 'What do I do?'

'What you're told, My Lord,' she retorted. 'Nothing else.'

He made singing hinnies and 'awesome' was too small a word for it. There was no explaining it. Either he was a natural-born cook or...

Or Jeanie was the world's best teacher. She certainly was good. She stood and instructed as he rubbed the butter into flour, as he made the perfect batter, as he heated the griddle on the stove, greased it with lard and finally popped his hinnie on to cook. It hissed and spluttered and rose. He flipped it over and it was done. Perfection! He placed it on a plate in the range's warming drawer and went on to make another, feeling about ten feet tall.

Closing a million-dollar deal against a business rival had never felt this good.

And then, when the last hinnie was on the plate, Jeanie put a teapot, mugs and butter and jam on a plate.

'My sitting room or yours?' she asked and that was a statement to give a man hope as well. He'd never been in Jeanie's tiny apartment. He'd seen it on the plans, a bedroom with a small living space specifically designed for a housekeeper. To be invited… Boundaries were certainly being shifted.

The castle was magnificent, lavish, amazing. Jeanie's apartment…wasn't. He stepped through the door and blinked. Gone were the opulent colours, drapes, rugs, furnishings of the ancient and historical treasure that was Duncairn Castle. This was just…home.

The dogs bounded in before him and nosedived to the hearth. The fire was crackling, emitting a gentle heat. The room was faded, homey, full of books and magazines and odds and sods: sea-shells in chipped bowls, photos in unmatched frames, ceramic dogs and the odd shepherdess—what was it with ceramic shepherdesses?—an old cuckoo clock, squashy furniture... All discards, he thought, from the rest of the castle, removed as Eileen had spent a fortune on redecorating.

He thought of his magnificent living quarters upstairs and suddenly it had lost its appeal.

'Get your cooking into you before it's cold,' Jeanie told him, still smiling, so he sat in one of her squashy armchairs and he ate four singing hinnies and drank two cups of tea, and Jeanie sat on the mat with the dogs and ate two singing hinnies and drank one cup of tea and then they were done.

Done? Jeanie cleared the cups and lifted the tray to one side. To safety? The world steadied—waiting to see what would happen?

The way he was feeling... She was so... Jeanie. There was no other word to describe her. Jeanie.

He slid down onto the mat beside her. The action was deliberate. One more boundary crossed?

He shouldn't be pushing boundaries. He, of all people, knew how important boundaries were, but maybe this one could be…stretched?

'Jeanie,' he said softly and he reached out and took her hand, not the hand wearing the wedding ring because for some reason the wedding ring was not where promises were to be made, but her right hand where lay the heavy signet of the Duncairn line.

'Jeanie,' he said again, and then, because he couldn't help himself, 'I'd really like to kiss you. No pressure. If you say no, then I won't ask you again.'

'Then I'd best say yes,' she said, softly, amazingly, wonderfully. 'Because I can't stand it one moment longer. I'd really, really like it if you kissed me.'

She was out of her mind. She should not be doing this—she should not!

She was and she had no intention of stopping.

They were on the rug before the fire. His hands cupped her face, he looked into her eyes for a

long, long moment, the world held its breath—
and then he drew her mouth to his and kissed her.

And she'd never been kissed like this. Never.
It was as if she'd found her home. Her centre.
Her heart.

There was all the tenderness in the world in his
kiss, and yet she could feel the strength of him,
the heat, the need. The sheer arrant masculinity
of him.

How could a kiss be a life changer? How could
a kiss make her feel she'd never been alive until
this moment?

How could a kiss make her feel as if her world
were melting, the outside fading to nothing, that
everything were disappearing except this man,
this moment, this kiss?

The heat...the strength...the surety... For that
was what it was, she thought in the tiny part
of her mind that was still available for rational
thought. Surety?

Home.

She was twenty-nine years old. She'd spent
twenty-nine years failing at this relationship business. She'd had a weak mother, a bully for a father, a husband who was no more than a mirror

of his family's business, then another who was vain and selfish and greedy.

This man might be all those things underneath, she thought, but there was no hint of it in his kiss. Her head should override what her body was telling her, what his kiss was telling her, but this kiss couldn't be ignored. This kiss was making her body feel as if it were no longer hers.

Rightly or wrongly, all that mattered was that, for this moment, Alasdair McBride wanted her and she wanted him, as simple as that. One man, one woman and a desire so great that neither could pull back. Sense had no place here. This desire was as primeval as life itself and she'd gone too far to pull back.

Too far to pull back? That was crazy. It was only a kiss. She could break it in a moment.

But she had no intention of breaking it. This kiss was taking her places she'd never been, places she hadn't known existed. Her hands had somehow found their way to his hair, her fingers sliding through the thick thatch of jet black, her hands drawing him closer so she could deepen... deepen...

She heard a tiny sound from far away and she

thought, That's me. Moaning with desire? What sort of dumb thought was that?

Dumb maybe, but the time for asking questions was over. If this moment was all she had of this man, her body knew she'd take it.

Weak perhaps? Stupid? Was it Jeanie being passive? Was this the Jeanie of old?

No. She felt her world shift and shift again and she knew this was no passive submission. Her hands held him even tighter and then tugged until his arms came around her and he drew her up to him, so his dark eyes could gleam into hers.

'Jeanie McBride, can I take my wife to bed?'

If the dogs hadn't been there, they might have made love right where they were—he certainly wanted to—but the dogs were gazing on with interest and, even though they were only dogs, it was enough to make a man take action.

Or maybe it was because he wanted to take this woman to bed with all the honour he could show her? Maybe this moment was too important to rush?

He wasn't sure what the reason was. Hell, his brain was mush, yet he knew enough to gather her into his arms and sweep her against his chest and carry her up the great, grand staircase to his rooms, to his bedroom, to the massive four-poster bed that was the place the Earls of Duncairn had taken their brides for generations past.

His bride?

She'd married him a month ago and yet a month ago she hadn't felt like this. He hadn't felt like this. As if this was his woman and he'd claim her and honour her and protect her from this day forth.

What had changed?

Nothing…and everything.

He'd spent the past month watching her. He'd come to her with preconceptions, prejudiced beyond belief by her marriage to his cousin. Those prejudices had been smashed by Jeanie, by her laughter, her courage, by everything about her. Every little thing.

He'd spent a month waiting for this new image to crack. Waiting for the true Jeanie to emerge.

It hadn't happened, or maybe…maybe it had. For the image he'd built up was a woman with a brave heart and an indomitable spirit.

What he held in his arms now was a woman of fire. A woman who, as he laid her down on his bed, as he hauled off his sweater and drew her to him, took the front of his shirt in her two hands and ripped…

'If you knew how long I've wanted to do this,' she murmured. And then she stopped because his chest was bare and she was gazing at him in awe…and then shifting just slightly so she could kiss…

She was adorable, he thought. She was stunning, beautiful, wild. She still had a smear of flour on her face from cooking. He'd never seen anything so beautiful in his life.

'If you've wanted to see me naked,' he said and he couldn't get his voice steady for the life of him, 'how do you think I've wanted to see you?'

And then she smiled, a smile of sheer transparent happiness, a smile that shafted straight to his heart.

Jeanie woke as the first rays of light crept over the sea through the window.

She woke and she was lying in the arms of the man she loved.

The knowledge almost blindsided her. She couldn't move. She could hardly breathe. She was lying tucked under his arm. He was cradling her—even in sleep? Her skin was against his skin. She could feel his heartbeat.

Her man. It was a feeling so massive it threatened to overwhelm her.

When she was young she'd loved Rory, large, dependable Rory, who'd wanted to please and protect her—as long as it hadn't interfered with his routine. She had loved him, she thought, but never like this. Never with this overwhelming sense of belonging.

For a short time she'd also thought she'd loved Alan. How long had it taken her to find the true Alan under the sham of the charming exterior? Too long.

But now... With Alasdair...

True waters run deep?

Where had that saying come from? She didn't know. She didn't even know if she had it right, but the words came to her now and she felt almost overwhelmed by their rightness.

This man was deep, private, a loner. She knew the story of his parents. She knew from Eileen about his solitary childhood and she'd learned more from him.

And now... She'd learned more in the past hours than she could even begin to understand.

He'd wanted her but this was more than that. The words he'd murmured to her through the night, the way he'd held her, the way he'd looked at her…

He'd shed his armour, she thought. Her great warrior had come home.

'Penny for them.' His voice startled her. It was still sleepy, but there was passion behind the huskiness. There was tenderness, too, and she thought last night wasn't just…last night. The armour was still discarded.

He was still hers.

'I was feeling like we should advertise singing hinnies as the world's new aphrodisiac,' she managed. 'Known only to us.'

'Let's keep it that way,' he said and gathered her closer. 'Just between us. It feels…excellent. Jeanie…'

'Mmm?' She lifted her face so she was pillowed on his chest. She liked his chest. As chests went, his was truly magnificent. The best?

'I don't know if I'm going to be any good at this.'

'At…'

'At marriage.'

She thought about that for a moment, assembling ideas and discarding them until she found the right one.

'Just lucky we're not, then.'

'We are.'

'No.' She pushed herself up so she was looking down at him, into his beautiful dark eyes, so she could see him clearly, all of him. He was her husband, her body was screaming at her—but she knew he wasn't.

'Alasdair, I've been down that path,' she said, slowly but surely, knowing that, no matter what her body was telling her, what she said was right. 'Twice now I've taken wedding vows and meant them. This time we spoke them but we didn't mean them. They were lies from the start so maybe that's the way it's meant to be. We've made the vows but now we need to prove them. We shouldn't even think of marriage before... unless...we fall in love.'

'Jeanie, the way I feel—'

'Hush,' she told him and put a finger to his lips. 'We both feel,' she told him. 'And maybe for you it's the first time, but for me... Alasdair, if this is for real, then it has to feel real. I won't have you held to me by vows we made when we were under duress. Let's leave this for a year.'

'A year…' He shook his head, his eyes darkening. He lifted one of her curls and twisted it and the sensation of the moving curl was enough to drive her wild all by itself. 'I have news for you. I don't think I can wait a minute.'

She was struggling to keep her voice even, to say what needed to be said. 'That's the way I feel, too, and I think… I think that's okay.'

'It has to be okay—wife.'

'No.' She drew back, still troubled. She had to make him see. 'I'm not your wife, Alasdair. For now I'm your lover, and I'd like… I'd like to stay your lover. Last night was…'

'Mind-shattering,' he said and she wanted to melt but she mustn't. She mustn't.

'We didn't go into last night with vows, though,' she managed. 'Alasdair…'

'Jeanie?'

He was driving her wild with wanting, but she had to say it. 'If at the end of the year we still want to marry, then…then we can think about it, but no pressure. We're not married until then.'

'So we're merely lovers?'

'I don't think merely comes into it.'

'Neither do I,' he said and he smiled and tugged her back to him. 'Maybe you're right,' he told her.

'A year of self-enforced courtship. A year where I'm locked in Duncairn Castle with my Jeanie, and at the end—'

'I'm not your Jeanie, and we'll worry about the end at the end.'

'But for the next few moments?'

And finally she managed to smile. Finally she let herself relax and savour being where she most wanted to be in the world. 'Let's just take each few moments as they come.'

'Starting now?'

And he smiled back at her, a dark, dangerous smile that had her heart doing back flips. He tugged her closer and he didn't need to wait for a response.

'Yes,' she breathed and then she could scarcely breathe at all.

CHAPTER NINE

LIFE HAD TO RESTART, a new norm had to be established, the world had to realign on its axis.

Lovers but not husband and wife?

It was working, Jeanie conceded as week followed week, as summer faded to autumn, as the castle settled to its new routine. Duncairn guests were now welcomed by a host as well as a hostess. Alasdair drew back on his visits to Edinburgh. He still worked during the day, sometimes from dawn, but at five every afternoon he kitted himself out in full highland regalia and came down the massive stairway to greet their guests.

Their guests. That was what it felt like. It was even fun, Jeanie conceded, sitting in the great library watching guests sipping their whisky, listening to Alasdair draw them out, listening to them tell of their travels, watching them fall under his spell.

It was also excellent for business. Although she nobly didn't advertise it, it was soon all over the web that the Earl of Duncairn Castle greeted his guests in person, and bookings went up accordingly.

'By the time you get your castle back it might be paying for itself,' she teased him that night.

For the nights were theirs. Their lives had fallen into a pattern. They walked the dogs at midday or when there was a break in the weather. They greeted the guests together. They had a brief dinner together. They came together at night.

Every night he was hers.

'We'll get the castle valued and add to your wages accordingly,' he told her. 'You needn't worry about the effort you're putting in not being appreciated.'

'I'm not worried about value.'

'You should be.'

But how to explain to him she didn't give a toss? How to say that she was living for the moment, and if, at the end of the year, this wasn't a marriage, then she'd not want anything to remind her of what could have been?

For she'd fallen in love, she conceded, as the weeks wore on. Alasdair might be able to hold himself apart, segment his life into times he could spend with her and times he couldn't, but there was no way she could.

He'd thought this could be a marriage, but Jeanie knew what bad marriages were, and she wanted more.

Did he think of her at all when he was elbow deep in his endless paperwork, phone calls, negotiations, flying trips to Edinburgh, fast international flights for imperative meetings? she wondered.

Did he fly back to her thinking, I want to get back to Jeanie? Or did he fly back thinking he had to get back to fulfil the stipulations of his grandmother's will?

At night, held in his arms, cocooned in the mutual passion, he felt all hers. But at dawn he was gone again.

She rose each day and got on with her work but she couldn't help listening for when the dogs' pressure got too much and she'd hear his study door open.

'Walk?'

How could she ever say no? It'd be like cutting her heart from her body. She donned her mac and her walking boots, they set off in whatever direction the dogs led them and she thought as she walked that she'd never been happier.

Except…

Except this was still compartmentalised. While they walked they talked of the castle, of the guests they'd had the night before, of the eagles, the otters, the wild things that crossed their path.

She tried, a few times, to ask about his work. Each time he answered politely, telling her what she wanted to know but no more.

The message was clear. His work was one compartment. She was another.

In those times she knew he wasn't hers completely. She could see it in his eyes—this was a midday walk between business sessions. His mind was on deals, plans, business she had no part in.

And she was part of his plans for the castle. As the weeks wore on she realised that. His decision to dress and come down to greet their guests was a business decision and a good one. She was part of that section of his business dealings but not the rest.

'I should be happy,' she told the dogs, because there was no one else to talk to. 'How many wives know their husband's business?'

She'd known Rory's—he'd bored her to snores with details of every last fish.

She'd been forced to know Alan's. He'd involved her in it to the point where she'd thought she was drowning.

Alasdair kept his business separate. She thought…she guessed…there was something worrying him about the business but she wasn't permitted to know what.

'It's his right to keep to himself,' she told the dogs. 'We could still… We might still be married, even if…'

Even if…

'He has less than a year to let me in,' she whispered. She was sitting by her hearth, supposedly reading, but she'd given the book up to hug the dogs. She needed hugging. It was late at night, she was tired and soon she'd go to bed but she could hear the distant murmur of Alasdair on the phone. Who was he talking to? Who knew?

Should she go to bed and wait?

'Of course I will,' she told the dogs. She had to be up early in the morning to get the guests' breakfasts, but, no matter how early she rose, Alasdair would rise earlier.

Ten more months to make a marriage?

'It's not going to work,' she said bleakly.

'So tell him,' she told herself.

'How can I?' She hugged the dogs tighter. 'How can I?' she asked them again. 'He's given me so much…how can I ask for more?'

It was working better than he'd thought possible. Somehow he seemed to have succeeded at this marriage business. Somehow he'd got it right.

For it was working. He spent his days immersed in doing what he'd been doing ever since his grandfather had taken him into the company's headquarters. That had always been his way of blocking out…life? He'd hated his parents' life, the life he'd been born to. His engagement to Celia had been an unmitigated disaster. When he'd realised how much she'd taken from him and how stupid he'd been, he'd backed into his world of business and he loved it. The cut and thrust of the financial world, where he knew the odds, where he held the cards, where he knew when to play and when to walk away… It was where he wanted to be.

The financial leaks he was dealing with now were troubling but intriguing. They were taking most of his attention, but gloriously, unexpectedly, Jeanie was fitting into the edges. She didn't intrude. She kept to herself but when he wanted her she was there. His perfect woman...

And then Elspeth dropped her bombshell.

If Jeanie Lochlan was Alasdair's perfect wife, Elspeth was his perfect secretary. She was the one person in his business world he trusted absolutely, and when she rang one afternoon and asked could she see him, the answer had to be 'of course'. The chopper was in Edinburgh. 'It'll be quicker if I come to you,' she told him. 'I need to talk face-to-face.'

The vague worries he'd been confronting for the past few weeks coalesced into a knot of trouble.

'I'll talk when I get there. There are too many ears in this place.' She disconnected and he stared at nothing.

The dogs were waiting for their walk and Jeanie was waiting with them. He joined her and he walked but his mind was all over the place.

'Is something wrong?' Jeanie asked as they reached the clifftops and he realised he hadn't spoken since they'd left the castle.

'I… No. My secretary's flying in at two. If needs be, can we put her up for the night?'

'Of course.'

'Thank you.'

'It's your castle,' she said gently, but he was no longer listening. He was playing scenarios out in his mind. Something was badly wrong. He knew it.

'Can I help?' she asked and he shook his head again and managed a smile.

'That'd be like me offering to fix your burned scones.'

'You can share my burned scones,' she told him, but she said it so lightly he hardly heard and his mind was off on tangents again.

She said little more. They returned to the house. She headed for the kitchen and closed the door behind her. He hesitated and then followed her.

'Jeanie, I might not be down to play host this evening.'

'We can cope without you,' she said, giving him a bright smile. 'The dogs and I put on a glorious welcome all by ourselves.'

'You lack the kilt.'

'We lack the title, too,' she said and her smile became a little more relaxed. 'The punters want to see the Earl of Duncairn, but they'll have to cope with portraits today. Isn't that the chopper landing?'

It was. He nodded and headed out to see it land.

He'd been right to be worried. Elspeth was distressed. As soon as he met her he could see the rigidity in her face, the fact that this was bad. He led her inside.

'Can I get you some tea? Jeanie could make us—'

'I don't want your wife bothered. Does she know about the business?'

'No.'

'Then let's leave it like that. The less people who know about this, the better. Alasdair, it's Don.'

'Don?' His grandmother's friend? 'What on earth…?'

'You know your grandparents gave him total trust? Last month you asked for the accounts to be audited, for everything your grandmother oversaw to be checked to make sure there weren't any gaps that hadn't been filled. The accounts that went through your grandmother's office were the only ones not subject to company scrutiny. Now it seems…' She took a deep breath. 'It seems you were right in your suspicions. You've been wondering for years how the Antica Corporation seem to be second-guessing us. They haven't been guessing. There's been an income stream from them flowing straight to Don's bank account.'

'Straight…'

'Well, not straight.' Elspeth handed over a folder. 'He couldn't do that, because the tax people would have caught him, so he's been streaming cash through the company accounts. Until Eileen's death the order's always been to leave Don's affairs to Don—maybe it was a measure of your grandparents' trust in him. So Don's financial dealings with the company have been audited for the first time ever. He's hidden it incredibly carefully. They've had to probe and probe, but finally it's exposed, and it's a hornet's nest. There's talk of insider trading—Don's been buying shares of companies we've dealings with and he's been buying them with money coming from Eileen's charity funds. There's so much… This has ramifications as far as the eye can see. The auditors want to call in the police. They need to talk to you but I thought it best I talk to you first.'

* * *

She watched them leave.

'I'll be back in a couple of days,' Alasdair said curtly, his face blank.

'What's wrong?'

'It's nothing to concern you. Apologise to the guests.'

Fine, she told herself. Life went on. She didn't need him.

She greeted the guests. She took the dogs for another walk. She made dinner for herself and had to force herself to eat, but the look on his face stayed with her. And with it came other doubts.

It's nothing to concern you.

She'd thought she had a marriage.

No, she conceded as the night wore on to the small hours and sleep wouldn't come. Until this afternoon she'd tried to pretend she had a marriage but as he'd left, with his face still impassive, revealing nothing of the turmoil she guessed was underneath, she'd felt…

Ill.

'Unless he comes back and tells me about it…' she whispered to the dogs, but she knew he wouldn't.

Because reality was finally sinking in.

They didn't have a marriage at all.

* * *

What followed was messy, nasty, heartbreaking. At least Eileen wasn't alive to see it, Alasdair thought. He wouldn't press charges—how could he? It'd make the company seem lax, and as well as that…it'd show the world he'd trusted.

Do not trust.

'Thank God I have Jeanie,' he told himself as the auditors unravelled the web of financial deceit and he saw the full extent of the betrayal of his grandparents' trust. 'Thank God I can go back to Jeanie. I can trust her. Separation of worlds is the only way to go. If I keep our lives separate, it'll work. It's the only way it can.'

He was away for two days. He returned late in the afternoon, the chopper flying in low from the east, setting him down and taking off almost as soon as he'd cleared the blades.

Jeanie was working in the kitchen. She saw the chopper land through the window. She let the dogs out and watched them race hysterically towards him. She watched him set down his bulging briefcase so he could greet them—and she thought maybe she should be doing the same.

The little wife, welcoming her husband home after his foray into the big, bad world.

He'd gone away looking as if he'd been slugged with a shock that was almost unbearable. He hadn't phoned. He'd told her nothing.

She wiped her hands slowly on the dishcloth and went to the door to greet him.

He looked exhausted. He looked…bleak. She wanted to put her arms around him and hug—but he was still in his business suit. His face said he still belonged to that other world.

And then he saw her waiting, and his face changed.

She saw it. He'd left here shocked and disoriented. Something bad had happened—she didn't have to be Einstein to figure that out. He'd been immersed in whatever it was for two days, and now he was home.

Now she watched him slough off whatever had made him look as if he'd come back from a war and turn into Alasdair. Into the man who took her to his bed.

His face creased into the smile she knew and loved. He reached her in three long strides, he had her in his arms and he swung her round and round as if she were a featherweight rather than a slightly too-curvy housekeeper who liked her own cooking.

His face radiated pleasure, and when finally he stopped swinging he set her down, cupped her face and kissed her.

A girl could drown in that kiss.

Not. She would not. For somewhere in the back of her head there was a place where passion couldn't reach. And it was ringing alarm bells that she'd heard before.

Once upon a time she'd fancied she was in love with Rory. He'd been the answer to her prayers, she'd been joyous when he'd asked her to marry him, but a tiny part of her had voiced doubts.

Do you want to spend the rest of your life cleaning his fish and watching football on the telly?

She'd ignored the voice. And then with Alan... That same little voice as she'd left the island with him, as she'd headed off to the world she'd dreamed of, the same voice had been whispering...

What does a man like this want with a girl like me? This doesn't make sense. Why is Eileen looking like she's worried?

And now that same dratted voice was no longer whispering. It was shouting.

*He's in trouble and he's not telling me. I'm just
the little wife, not to be worrying her head about
such things. I'm just the cook and bottle washer,
and a warm body in his bed.*

'Alasdair,' she managed. 'What's happened?'

'Nothing that need concern you. Give me thirty
minutes. I need to make a couple of calls and I'll
be with you.'

'I'll be in the kitchen.'

He must have heard the strain in her voice. 'Is
something wrong?'

'Nothing that need concern you.'

'Jeanie—'

'Go and get changed,' she told him, feeling suddenly weary beyond belief. 'I'll see you when
you're ready.'

The calls stretched to an hour. He hadn't meant
them to, but if Don's fraud wasn't to hit the front
pages of the financial papers, there were people
he had to placate. He'd used an outside auditor
and outside audit firms had their own leaks. Ru-
mours were swirling and they had to be settled.

The legal problems were another matter. They
were still a minefield to be faced.

When finally he reached the kitchen he was beyond exhaustion. Jeanie was waiting. He smiled at seeing her, hoping like hell she wouldn't ask what was wrong again, immeasurably thankful for her presence.

She was making shortbread, pressing dough into wooden moulds with thistles carved into them, then tapping the shaped dough out onto trays. He sank into a chair and watched. She let him be for a while. Three moulds. Four.

'Do you enjoy making them?' It was a bit of an inane question but he was feeling inane right now.

'I'm good at it.' She looked down at the perfect circles. 'It's supposed to be what a good Scottish housewife does.'

That was a jarring note. 'You'd rather be doing something else?'

'Learning to fly,' she said, unexpectedly. She gestured to the window where, in the distance, he could see the eagles soaring in the thermals. 'Like those guys. But each to his own. They fly. I make shortbread. Alasdair, I need to ask you again. What's wrong?'

'Just a problem at headquarters.'

'A big problem.' It wasn't a question.

'Maybe.' His tone said no more questions.

She looked at him for a long moment and then filled a couple more moulds. The shortbread shapes looked beautiful, perfect circles with a thistle etched on top. He hardly noticed.

It was enough that she was here. That was all he wanted, Jeanie, a safe haven where he could bury the outside world.

He glanced outside at the eagles and thought he was very glad she wasn't out there flying. He wanted her here.

A good Scottish housewife?

'Alasdair, let me in,' she said and his thoughts focused. The almost animal instinct to relax, to let himself be…just disappeared.

'How do you mean?'

'You know what I mean.' She took a deep breath and steadied. 'Something's happened, something bad. I could read Elspeth's face. I could see your shock. You left looking like death. I've heard nothing from you for two days and you return looking like you've been through the wringer. You say it's nothing to concern me. You have me worried.'

'Don't worry.'

'You lie in my arms every night and I shouldn't worry for you?'

He didn't want this conversation. He was too tired. 'Jeanie, you're separate. You're here, you're part of this place and that's all that matters. I can't believe what we've managed to forge. If you knew how much I've been aching to come back to you...'

'You're back and you're hurting.' Her tone was neutral. 'But you don't want to tell me why?'

'You're not part of that world.'

'And you don't want me to know about it?'

'I don't want to have to trust...'

And as soon as he said it, he knew he'd killed something. He saw it in her face. He might just as well have slapped her.

If he hadn't been so tired, he would have phrased it better, thought of some way round it, thought of how he could deflect it. But the words had been said, and they seemed to hang over his head, like a sword, about to come crashing down.

'You don't trust,' she said, softly now, as if she, too, feared the sword.

'I do. I can.'

'You mean you can trust me with the parts of your world you allow me to share. The part that likes hinnies and shortbread and walking the dogs and holding me at night. But there are parts you won't entrust to me.'

'No. I…'

'Are they state secrets? Stuff that'd bring down countries, stuff worth so much secret agents might torture me to make me confess?'

He managed a smile. 'Hardly. Jeanie—'

'Then what?' She ran a hand through her curls, leaving a wash of flour she didn't notice. 'What's so important?'

'It's just that our worlds are different.' He was too tired to explain. He couldn't get it right. 'I don't interfere with your life—'

'As I see it, you've interfered a lot.' Her voice was calm, but the shuttered look was down. 'You married me to save your inheritance. You're walking in and out of my world as you like, but it's all one-way.'

'You don't want to be part of my world.'

'Part of your business world?'

'Right. It has nothing to do with you.'

'And if it did…I'd likely betray something? Do you really think that?'

'No.' It was he who was raking his hair now. He was so tired he couldn't get this right, but he had to. What to say?

And in desperation he said it. 'Jeanie, I've fallen in love with you.' The words were out and they didn't sound so bad. In fact, they sounded okay. Good, even. This house, this woman, this home... 'This is everything I want,' he told her. 'And I don't want to mess with that.'

He'd just told a woman he loved her. It was big. It was momentous—but Jeanie was staring at him as if he'd offered poison. 'So...sharing might mess with it?'

'I don't know,' he said honestly. 'Maybe. All I know is that I love what we have here. Can you not just accept that?'

'I already have accepted it.' But her voice was dead. Whatever response he'd been hoping for, he knew it wasn't this.

'You mean you love me?'

'No. Or maybe. But it doesn't matter. It can't matter.' She was looking stricken. She took two steps back from the table as if she needed to put distance between them. 'I mean I've been married before, Alasdair. Married, but not *married*. Married on just the terms you're offering.'

And that got him. 'How can you compare me to Alan?'

'Or Rory?' she added. 'I'm not comparing

men. I'm comparing marriages. They've been three very different…disasters but the same each time. They say some people go on repeating the same mistake for the rest of their lives. It's time I stopped.'

'Jeanie…'

'Rory was older than me,' she said, still in that cold, dead voice. He wanted to go to her but the look on her face was a shield all by itself. 'He was like my big brother. When my mam died, I was gutted but Rory stood up for me. He stood up to my bully of a father. He made me feel safe and when he married me I thought I was the luckiest woman on the island. The problem was, that's who I was. The little woman, to be protected. I never shared Rory's world. I was a tiny part of it. I was the woman who kept the home fires burning, who cleaned and cooked and worked for his parents, but when he wanted to talk he went out with the boys. I never knew anything that troubled him. I was his wife and I knew my place.'

'I don't—'

'Think you're like that? No? And then there was Alan.' She was talking fast now, her hands up as if to prevent him interrupting. Or taking her in his arms? Her hands said do neither. 'Alan blew me away with his fun, his exuberance, the way he embraced…everything. I was still young and I was stupid and I'd been bogged down by grief at Rory's death for so long that I fell for him like a ton of bricks. And when he asked me to marry him I was dazzled. But Alan, too, had his secrets. The biggest one was that he was up to his neck in debt. He was desperate for his grandmother to bail him out and he thought by marrying someone she was fond of he'd get her to agree. She did, but at what cost? I was trapped again, a tiny part of a life I couldn't share.'

'This is nothing like that.' He was on his feet now, angry. That she would compare him to his cousin…

'I know you're not.' Her voice softened. 'I know you're nothing like Alan. But you have your demons, too. You've let me close enough to see them, but, Alasdair, whether I see them or not is irrelevant. You won't share.'

'I want to be married. This can work.'

'You don't want to be married.' She shook her head, as if trying to work it out for herself. 'The thing is that I have a different definition of marriage from you. Marriage is supposed to be the joining together of two people—isn't it? That's what I want, Alasdair. That's what I dream of. But you…you see marriage as the joining together of the little bits you want to share.'

'You don't want to know about my business.'

'Maybe I don't,' she said slowly. 'But that's not what I'm talking about. You don't want to trust. You don't want to share because it'll make you somehow more exposed. And I don't want that sort of semi-commitment. More, I'll run a mile before I risk it. I'm sorry, Alasdair, but it has to end. The vows we took were only mock. You say you love me. It's a wonderful compliment but that's all it is—a compliment. We need to work out a way forward but the little loving we've been sharing isn't the way to go. It has to end and it will. Right now.'

He looked ill but she wouldn't allow herself to care. She mustn't. Something inside was dying but she couldn't let herself examine it. Like a wounded creature of the wild, she needed to be left alone. She wanted to find a place where she could hide.

To recover? How did she recover? She felt dead inside. Hopeless.

'Alasdair, you're too tired to take this in.' She

forced herself to sound gentle—to play the concerned wife? No. She was a concerned friend
now, she told herself. Nothing more. 'How long
since you slept?'

'I can't—'

'Remember? Go up and sleep. We'll talk later.'

'We'll talk now.' It was a possessive growl and
instinctively she backed away.

'Not now. There's nothing to say until you've
thought it through.'

'You won't leave while I sleep?'

'No.'

'And after that?'

'We'll talk tomorrow. Go to bed.'

'Jeanie...'

'Alasdair, I have guests arriving in half an hour
and I have work to do. Please...leave me be.'
She turned to put trays of her shortbread into
the oven.

If he came up behind her, she thought, if he
touched her, how could she keep control? She
was so close to the edge...

But he didn't come. She waited, every nerve in
her body, every sense tuned to the man behind
her. If he touched her...

She'd break. She'd said what she had to say.

She'd meant it but her body didn't mean it. Her body wanted him.

She wanted him, but the cost was too high. The cycle had to be broken, right here, right now.

Please… It was a silent prayer and in the end she didn't know whether it was for him to leave or for him to stay. Please…

And in the end who knew whether the prayer was answered?

He left.

He was too tired to think straight. He was too tired to fight for what he wanted.

The mess in Edinburgh had needed a week to sort, but, with only twenty-eight nights away from the castle permissible under the terms of the will, he'd had to get home. So he'd worked through, forty-eight hours straight.

His head was doing weird things. It was as if Jeanie's words had been a battering ram, and he'd been left concussed.

It must be exhaustion, he told himself. He should have stayed another night in Edinburgh— he could have managed it in his schedule—but he'd wanted to get home.

To Jeanie.

She was downstairs and she wasn't coming up. She intended to sleep in her own apartment. He'd be going to bed alone.

Maybe it was just as well. He needed time to think. He had to get it sorted.

Maybe she was talking sense. Maybe the type of relationship she was demanding wasn't something he could give?

His head hurt.

He showered and his head didn't clear. The night was closing in. All he saw was fog.

He headed for his bedroom and there was a bowl of soup and toast and tea by his bed.

'Try to eat,' the note beside it said. 'Things will look better in the morning.'

How could they look better?

Was she talking about Don? About the betrayal?

He hadn't told her about Don. He hadn't let her close.

He stared down at the simple meal, thinking he wanted her to be here while he ate it.

He wanted her as an accessory to his life?

It was too hard. He couldn't make his mind work any more. He managed half the meal. He put his head on the pillow and slept.

* * *

She shouldn't have cooked for him. The little wife preparing supper for her businessman husband, home after a frantic two days at the office? Ha.

But this much was okay, she told herself. She'd waited until she heard the sound of his shower and then slipped his meal in unseen, as she'd done a hundred times for guests who'd arrived late, who hadn't been able to find a meal in town or who were ill or in trouble.

He was a guest, she told herself. That was the way it was now. He was a guest in the bed and breakfast she worked in. Nothing more.

CHAPTER TEN

HE WAS TROUBLED by dreams but still he slept, his body demanding the rest it so badly needed. He hadn't set his alarm and when he woke it was nine o'clock and he could hear the sound of guests departing downstairs.

He lay and let the events of the past two days seep back into his consciousness. He allowed them in piece by piece, assessing, figuring out what had gone wrong, how he could have handled things better.

The financial and legal mess Don had left would have ramifications into the future. He should let his mind dwell on that as a priority. Instead his brain skipped right over and moved on...

To Jeanie.

There was a scratch at the door. The dogs. He rose to let them in and found an envelope had been slipped under the door. Like a checkout slip from a hotel? *Thank you for your patronage—here's the cost?*

He snagged the envelope, let the dogs in and went back to bed. Abbot and Costello hit the covers with joy. He patted them but his pat was perfunctory.

'Nice to see you, too, guys. Settle.'

And they did settle, as if they, too, knew the contents of the envelope were important.

He lay back on the bed, reluctant to open it but it had to be done. It contained two pages of what looked like…a contract?

Note first.

Dear Alasdair,

You'll be worried by now that I'm going to leave. If I do, then of course things revert to their former disaster. I won't do that to you. Just because my emotional needs don't match yours, there's no need to bring down the Duncairn Empire.

Alasdair, your grandmother's will was fanciful—an old lady's wish born out of fondness for me. But she's already done so much for me—more than enough—so this is how it will be.

I'll stay until the end of the twelve months, as your housekeeper. I'll accept a decent wage, but that's all. At the end of the year I'll walk away and I'll take nothing. The following contract, signed by me and witnessed by the guy who delivered this morning's groceries, grants you every right to the castle.

I know Alan's creditors will still claim it, but you can then pay them out if you wish. Or not. It's nothing to do with me. All I want—and I do want this—is the dogs. Oh, and what's left of my whisky. I've given up the idea of selling it online so I'll be making awesome Christmas cakes for generations. That's my own little Duncairn Legacy.

Meanwhile, if you sign the contract, that's what it says and that's where we'll leave it. It's as professional as I can make it.

It's been lovely, Alasdair, but we should never have mixed business with pleasure. You're right—our lives are separate.

Oh, and your ring is in the safe in your grandmother's room. I have no right to it, and it's too precious to lose.

Yours back to being formal.

Jeanie

* * *

He lay and stared at the ceiling while the dogs settled, draped themselves over him, slept.

Our lives are separate.

Downstairs he heard Jeanie start to hoover. In a while she started to hum and then to sing.

If he didn't know better, he'd think she was happy. She wasn't. He'd lived in the same castle as this woman for almost two months. He could hear the note of determined cheerfulness. The courage.

She had a great voice, he thought inconsequenially. With the hoover in the background it was the best...

Jeanie...

Too precious to lose?

Hell.

The dogs were letting him go nowhere—or maybe it was his mind letting him go nowhere. What he'd learned in a crisis was to get all the facts before he made a move and he didn't have all the facts before him yet. Or he did, but they weren't in the proper order. He needed to marshal them, set them in a line, examine them.

But they wouldn't stay in line. They were jumping at him from every which way, and overriding all of them was the sound of Jeanie singing.

The contract fell off the coverlet, onto the floor. He let it lie.

Done. Dusted. Sorted. Jeanie had told him the end of this particular story. Move on.

It'd been all right when he'd thought he'd been buying her out, he thought savagely. Why wasn't it okay now?

His phone interrupted. It was his chief lawyer calling to talk about Don. Listening to what the man was telling him, he felt some relief—but suddenly the lawyer was talking about something else. Jeanie's bankruptcy?

What he told him made Alasdair pay more attention than all the details of Don's betrayal.

Why tell him this now? he demanded, but it had only been after a long examination of all the contracts that the lawyers had felt sure.

He disconnected feeling…discombobulated. Talk about complications! What was he going to do with this?

He needed to walk. He needed to get his mind clear before he talked to her.

'Come on, guys,' he told the dogs, tossing back the covers. 'Let's go discuss this with the otters.'

* * *

She hoovered every inch of the castle and then some. Halfway through the hoovering she heard Alasdair come down the stairs, the dogs clattering after him. She held her breath but she heard them head straight for the wet room. The back door slammed and then she heard silence.

He'd taken the dogs for a walk? Good.

'But I'm taking the dogs when I go,' she muttered and she tried to make herself sound angry but in the end all she felt like was crying.

But she would not cry. Not again. Not over a man—even if he was Alasdair. She had to keep it together and get the next ten months over with. For ten months she had to live in the castle so their mock marriage could stay intact. She had to stay sane.

She would.

She sniffed and sniffed again, and then walked determinedly to the back door. Alasdair and the dogs were over the brow of the first hill. Out of earshot? Excellent. She took a deep breath, stood on the top step and let fly.

'Don't you dare get attached to those dogs,' she yelled, to the departing Alasdair, to the world in general. 'They're mine. I don't have a right to your castle, but your grandma's dopey dogs are mine, and I'll fight for them.'

And the whisky?

'And the whisky, too,' she yelled but he was long gone and nobody heard.

She wouldn't cry. *She would not.*

Instead she went back inside and returned to her hoovering. 'Back to being the char,' she told herself and then she forced a mocking smile. 'But back to being your own woman as well. It's about time you learned how.'

He headed along the cliffs, to Craigie Burn, to the place where he and Jeanie had watched the otters. The dogs were wild with excitement, but then they were always wild with excitement. They raced deliriously around him but finally settled to his gentle amble, keeping him in sight but leaving him to himself. When he paused at the point where the burn cut him off from wild woods beyond, the dogs found a rabbit warren and started digging. Next stop China, he thought as he watched the dirt flying. Any Duncairn rabbit was safe from this pair. They were closer to burying each other than catching anything.

He left them be. He headed for the cottage, sa

on the rock above the water and stared at nothing in particular. He had things to be thinking, things to be working out, but his mind seemed to have gone into shutdown.

Jeanie had given him what he wanted—hadn't she? It was selfish to want more.

The dogs were yapping in the distance and he found himself smiling. Stupid dogs.

At the end of the year he wouldn't have them.

He could buy others. He could find dogs with a bit more intelligence.

He could find...another woman?

And there his thoughts stopped.

Another woman?

A wife?

He didn't want a wife. He wanted Jeanie.

Two different things.

But he'd treated her as...just a wife, he conceded, thinking of the past few weeks. *A housewife.* He'd played the businessman, and Jeanie was his appendage. Each had their clear delineation of responsibility. Each only interacted on a need-to-know basis.

Except Jeanie hadn't treated their marriage like that, he thought. She hadn't compartmentalised as he had. She'd welcomed him into her kitchen, into her bed, into her life.

She'd told him everything he wanted to know about this business, this island, her life. She'd opened herself to him, whereas he…

He'd done what would work. He'd resisted the temptation to trust because trust only led to trouble.

A movement by the water's edge caught his eye. Welcoming the diversion from thoughts that were taking him nowhere, he let himself be distracted. The pocket of his hiking jacket always held a pair of field glasses. He hauled them out and focused.

A pair of sea otters were at the water's edge beneath him, devouring the end of what looked like the remains of a rather large fish. He watched caught by their beauty and their activity, welcoming the diversion.

What was a group of sea otters called? A raft? He found himself wondering why.

And then he found out. The fish finished, the otters slipped back into the water and drifted lazily out midstream. They stayed hard against each other and he focused his glasses to see more clearly.

They were linked. Hand in hand? Paw in paw? They floated on the surface, their faces soaking up the rays of the weak autumn sun, replete, relaxed, ready for sleep? Together they made a raft of two otters. Their eyes were closed. They were only two, but their raft was complete.

Jeanie would like to see this.

And then he thought: I can show her—but at the end of the year she'll walk away.

Because he couldn't trust? No, because he didn't want to trust. He didn't want to risk…

Risk what? Losing his business? She'd saved that for him. This estate? It'd survive as well.

What, then?

Did trust have to mean betrayal?

In his world, it did. His parents had shown him no loyalty whatsoever. They'd dumped him whenever they could. He'd had one disastrous engagement, which had ended in betrayal. He'd been humiliated to the core. And now Don… An old family friend. A man his grandparents had trusted completely.

He'd lost through betrayal. His parents. His fiancée. Don. The hurt from his parents was ongoing. His father had died without ever showing him affection. His mother…she was with someone in the US. Someone fabulous, someone rich, someone who didn't want anything to do with her past.

And now... If his grandmother had known about Don, it would have broken her heart, he thought. Oh, Eileen, you should have learned. Counter betrayal by not trusting. Don't leave yourself open to that devastation.

Eileen had loved Jeanie. She'd trusted her completely.

Was that why she'd engineered this marriage—because she'd trusted Jeanie to love her grandson? What an ask.

The otters were drifting further downstream, seemingly asleep, seemingly oblivious to their surroundings. Were they pups? he wondered. A mother and her offspring? A mating pair?

Did otters mate and stay mated? He needed to find out.

He watched them float and found himself thinking that what he was seeing was perfect trust. They were together and that seemed all that mattered.

But...they were floating towards the point where the burn met the incoming sea.

The burn was running gently, but the sea was

not so gentle. There must have been a storm out in the Atlantic not long since, because the sea was wild. The breakers were huge and the point where the waves washed into the mouth of the burn was a mass of white water.

The otters were almost there.

Were they pups? Didn't they know? Dumb or not, he found himself on his feet, staring helplessly at them, wanting to yell...

His glasses were still trained on their heads. Just as they reached the point where the wash of surf could have sucked them in, he saw one stir and open its eyes...

What followed was a swift movement—a nudge? They were both awake then, diving together straight into the wash, surfacing on a wave, cruising on its face across the surf—then back into the safety and relative calm of the burn.

He watched them glide sleekly back up the burn, past him, then drift together again, once more forming a raft—then close their eyes and proceed to do it all over again.

Trust...

And suddenly it was as if invisible cords were breaking from around him. He felt light, strange—free.

Thoughts came after the sensation. It was as if his body already knew what his mind would think. He had to watch the otters for a while as his mind caught up.

But catch up it did.

The otters trusted.

Rafted together, two lots of senses looked onto the outside world. Who knew if otters hunted together, but, if they did, two must be able to work more effectively than one. Two had devoured a truly excellent salmon that might well have been too much for one. Rafted together, they seemed a larger animal, a bigger presence to possibly deter predators.

Rafted together, they could have fun?

Fun.

Trust. Dependence.

Love.

The thoughts were almost blindsiding him. He wasn't sure what to do with them but when he finally rose there was only one thing he knew for certain.

He had to share.

CHAPTER ELEVEN

'COME AND SEE.'

Three words. He said them but he hardly knew whether she'd accept or not.

He'd brought the dogs home, settled them, given them a bone apiece. He'd fetched another pair of field glasses and then put a rug into a backpack and a bottle of wine. Hopeful, that. Then he'd searched for Jeanie. She was in the library, wiping her whisky bottles clean. She was polishing…for the sake of polishing?

'Come where?' She didn't turn to face him. There must be a smear on the bottle she had in her hand. It was taking all her concentration.

'To Craigie Burn. I need you to come, Jeanie. Please.'

She shouldn't come. She shouldn't go anywhere near this man. He…did things to her. He touched her without touching her.

He made her feel exposed and raw, and open

to a pain that seemed to have been with her all her life.

'Please,' he said again and she set down the whisky bottle with a steadying clink.

'The guests arrive at four. I'll be back by then?'

'You will.' It was a promise and it steadied her.

'Give me five minutes to change.'

What did he want? Why was she going? She was an idiot, she told herself as she went to fetch a sweater and coat. A blind idiot.

Come and see, he'd said, so she went.

'I was born a fool,' she told herself as she headed for the back door where he stood waiting. 'Have you no idea how to defend yourself?'

Come and see, he'd said and she had no weapons at all.

The otters were gone. Of course they were; they were wild creatures who went where they willed. They'd hunted and eaten and moved on. Who knew where they were now? Alasdair stood on the cliff and surveyed the water below.

No otters.

It didn't matter.

'Come and see…what?' Jeanie asked beside him. They'd walked here in almost total silence.

Who knew what she was thinking? It was enough that she trusted him to take her here, he thought. He wouldn't ask more.

'I want you to see the otters,' he told her. 'They were here this morning. They're not here now but I still want you to see them.'

She looked at him in silence for a long moment. 'Right,' she said. 'You know they might not appear again for a week?'

'They'll appear if you close your eyes and let yourself see.'

There was another silence, longer this time. And then she closed her eyes.

'I'm watching.'

Trust…

It took his breath away. It was a small thing, doing what he'd asked, coming with him, closing her eyes on demand, but that she would put her trust in him…

He wanted to take her into his arms, tell her he loved her, sweep her into the moment.

Instead he made himself take his time. He spread his blanket on the ground, took her arms and pressed her gently to sit.

'What can you hear?'

'The burn,' she said, promptly. 'The water rippling down over the rocks. The waves in the distance. There's a bird somewhere…a plover? If it's thinking about swooping while I have my eyes closed…'

'It's not thinking about swooping. You're safe.'

'I trust you. Thousands wouldn't. What do you want me to see, Alasdair?'

And there was a note of restraint in her voice that told him this was hard for her. Trust was hard?

She had no reason to trust him. No reason at all.

'I want you to see the otters,' he told her, gently now. He sank down beside her and took her hand. He felt her stiffen, he felt the sharp intake of her breath and then he felt her consciously force herself to relax.

'Word picture?' she said and she had it. He had to smile. He might have guessed this woman would know what he was about.

'I watched them this morning,' he told her. 'Imagine them just below this overhang, on the great rock covered with weed. Two otters. I don't know if they were young or old, male or female, mother and cub, but I'm imagining…something in them was like us. Two creatures blessed with having all Duncairn as our domain.'

'I won't—'

'Stay with your eyes closed, Jeanie. Keep seeing the otters, but while you do I need you to listen to what I want to tell you. I need to say this first because I can't talk of the future without clearing the past. Jeanie, I would never marry you for the castle. I'm asking you to accept that. I've been thinking of this all night. Thinking it makes it impossible to ask…but today, looking at the otters, I thought, maybe I *can* ask you to trust. But before I ask… Jeanie, the castle is yours.'

Her forehead wrinkled. 'I don't understand.'

He put his finger to her lips. 'Hush, then. Hear me out. This has nothing to do with you or me. It's a legal opinion. I've had Duncairn's best legal minds look at the mess that Alan left you with. He assigned you his debt, he died and you were somehow lumbered with it. You'd signed contracts…'

'I know. I was stupid.'

'He was your husband. You weren't stupid, you were trusting and you were intimidated. But you were also conned. But the lawyers have demanded copies and it's taken time. The contracts contain pages of small print, but on all of them your name appears only on the first page. Did you read all those contracts?'

'I didn't even see the rest,' she confessed. 'Alan only ever gave me one page. There was no hint of more. He said it was so he could use the house Eileen had given us as security for business dealings. I thought…it was Alan's right—Eileen's gift had been to Alan.'

'Eileen wanted to keep you safe, but that's beside the point. The lawyers say there was no financial advantage to you included in the contracts Alan had you sign. If you'd initialled each page, if there was proof you'd read them in full, then the contracts could have held water, but as it is… Jeanie, those debts aren't binding. There was no need for you to be declared bankrupt. If Eileen had given you a decent lawyer instead of offering you a place here as housekeeper, she would have been doing you a much bigger service.'

'But I love it here.' She still had her eyes closed. She was feeling the salt in the autumn air, listening to the ocean, to the water rippling over the rocks. What he was saying seemed almost dreamlike. She didn't want to think of Alan and contracts and debt. Or even the castle. They all seemed a very long way away. 'What are our otters doing now?'

'They've just caught fish,' he told her. 'A fish apiece. They're eating them slowly, savouring them. They must be sated—the fishing must have been good this morning. Jeanie, we can discharge your bankruptcy right now. The lawyers are already instigating proceedings. As of now you're free of debt, and if we can manage to stay together for the next ten months, then Eileen's wishes are granted. You get the castle. I get the remainder.'

She had to force herself to focus. 'I don't want the castle. You're the Earl of Duncairn. It's your right.'

'I don't have rights. The otters are finishing their fish, right now. They're doing a little grooming.'

'I love watching otters groom. Are they sleek? Are they beautiful?'

'The sun's shining on their coats. The one on the left has fish caught in his whiskers. He's using his paws to get himself clean, then grooming his paws as well. How can we train the dogs to do that?'

'That's...my problem.'

'I'd like it to be ours.' He said it almost non-chalantly, as if it didn't matter at all. 'They've finished grooming now. They're slipping back into the water. They're slipping under, doing a few lazy circles, maybe getting rid of the last trace of fish. Jeanie, I had to tell you about the castle. I don't mean I'm reluctant to tell you. It's just that you need to know before…before I ask you something else.'

'Why?'

It was a tiny word, half whispered.

'Because what I'm about to say demands trust,' he told her. 'Because if I ask you to marry me properly, then you might think that I'm doing it now because of the castle. For castle, for keeps. I wouldn't do that, Jeanie.'

'I don't—'

'The otters have come together now,' he told her and he took her hands in his. She was shaking. Hell, *he* was shaking. She tugged away but when he went to release her she seemed to change her mind. Her hands held his as if he were an anchor in a drifting world.

'They're floating,' he told her. 'But the burn is running down to the sea. They'll end up on the rocks where the surf breaks.'

'They'll turn.'

'I know they will.' His grip on her hands tightened. What happened in the next few moments was so important—all his life seemed to be hanging in the balance. 'But look what they're doing now. They're catching paws. Catching hands.'

'I've seen them do that,' she whispered, unsure where he was going but willing to still see his otters. 'It's called rafting. A raft of otters.'

'So have I but I didn't get it until this morning,' he told her. 'I'm watching them float almost into the surf. They have their eyes closed, as yours are closed now, but one's aware. Just as the rocks grow sharp and jagged, just before they're in peril, his eyes fly open, and he moves and his partner's nudged and they dive away to safety. And then watch them, Jeanie. They disappear under the water, they glide unseen…and then they're upstream and they're rafting again and they're floating down, loving the water, loving the sun on their faces, but this time it's the other otter who stays aware, who does the nudging. Who keeps them both safe.'

'Why are you telling me this?' She seemed breathless. Her face was turned to the sun. Her eyes were still closed as if she didn't want to let go the vision.

'Because they've learned to trust, Jeanie,' he said softly. 'And because they trust, they can have fun. Because they trust, they can eat together, hunt together, float together. And as I lay on this rock this morning and I watched them, I thought of the way I've compartmentalised my life. I thought of how you've been hurt in the past by just such compartments and here I was doing it all over again. I've hurt you, Jeanie, and I'm sorry.'

He was finding it hard to keep talking. So much depended on this moment. So much…

'Jeanie, now, with the castle, you must know that it's yours,' he told her. 'You know the only way I can have any claim on it is to marry you properly so I need to say it upfront. For you need to know that I want to marry you no matter what you do. If you want to sell the castle to care for all the dogs of Europe, then it has to be okay with me. As long as you let me share your life. As long as you let me take your hand and let me float beside you.'

Her eyes were still closed. He was watching

her face and he saw a tiny tic move at the corner of her mouth. Revulsion? Anger?

'You want me to float?' she demanded at last.

'With me.'

'In the burn? You'd be out of your mind. It's freezing.'

And the tic was laughter. Laughter! 'Metaphorically,' he said, with all the dignity he could muster.

'You don't really want to float with me?'

'If you want to float, then I'll float,' he said heroically and the tic quivered again.

'In your kilt?'

'If you ask it of me.'

'For castle, for keeps,' she mused and he couldn't bear it.

'Jeanie, open your eyes.'

'I'm still watching otters. They're having fun.'

'We could have fun.'

'You'd want to share my whisky.'

'Guilty as charged. And your dogs. I'd want to share your dogs.'

'I might want more.'

'Okay.' He was ready to agree to anything. Anything at all. 'But...can we get smart ones?'

he suggested, cautiously, and then even more cautiously… 'And maybe eventually a bairn or two?'

The tic quivered. 'Bairns! With you spending thirty days a year away from the castle?'

'I've been thinking about that. Jeanie, I do need to travel to keep the company viable. I'd like the castle to stay as our home—if you're happy to share—but if I need to leave…would you fancy travelling with me?'

'Floating, you mean?'

'It would be my very great honour to keep you safe from rocks and rapids, but I'm looking forward now, Jeanie, and I can't see rapids. If you agreed to marry me, if we can both find it in ourselves to trust, then I can't see a rock in sight. But right now I'm thinking about flying.'

'Flying…'

'If you'd truly like to learn to fly—and you can't make shortbread forever—then flying's an option. Jeanie, what I've been doing for the last few days is complicated. I'll explain it all to you later, in all the detail you want, but, in a nutshell, Eileen's best friend in the company has betrayed her trust, a thousand-fold, leaving a legal and financial nightmare. That's why I had to leave in such a hurry. For a while I thought the foundations of the company might give, but we've done some massive shoring up, and this morning's legal advice is that we'll survive. The insider trading Don was involved in will fall on his head, not the company's. We might well need to adopt economies, however, so combining roles might be just what Duncairn Enterprises needs.'

'How…how do you mean?'

'Your role, for instance.' He wanted to tug her into his arms. It took an almost superhuman effort not to, but he had to keep control. So much hung on what he had to say right now.

'If you would like to reach for the sky,' he managed, 'how about a new role? Not Jeanie McBride, Alasdair's wife. How about Jeanie McBride, pilot and partner? You'd need lessons—lots of lessons—and that could be…fun?'

'Lessons?'

'Flying lessons. If that's your dream, Jeanie, I don't see why you shouldn't have it.'

'You'd teach me to fly?' Her eyes flew wide.

'Not me,' he said hurriedly. 'I'd sit in the passenger seat with my eyes closed. It's not a good look for a teacher. But we could find someone to teach you, and if you were flying, I'd be right with you. Trusting you like anything.'

She shook her head in wordless astonishment and he had to force himself to keep going. All he wanted to do was to kiss her, but he had this one chance. Don't blow it, he told himself. Say it like it is.

'It's not for castle, for keeps, Jeanie love,' he said, gently but urgently. 'If you agree…it's for *us*, for keeps. It's for us, for fun. For us, forever. Jeanie McBride, I love you. Whatever you do or say now, that's unchanged—I love you whatever you decide to do. But I do need to ask. Jeanie, I'd like to say our vows again, but this time for real. This time I'd like to say those vows aloud, and, if you let me, I'd like to mean them for the rest of our lives.'

There was a long, long silence. She blinked in the sunlight. Her gaze was a long, in-depth interrogation where he couldn't begin to guess the outcome.

'You'd trust me,' she said at last. 'With the bad things as well as the good?'

'I might try to protect—'

'No protection. Just trust.'

'Okay,' he said humbly. 'Trust first.'

'Really with the flying?'

'Really with the flying.' And then he added

honestly, 'Unless you end up stunt flying, in which case no love in the land is big enough.'

'Coward.'

'I'd rather be a chicken than a dead hen.'

She grinned at that. 'I can't see the Lord of Duncairn as a dead hen.'

'And you can't expect the Lord of Duncairn to be a complete doormat,' he agreed. 'I might try to protect, but I'll do my best to let you fly free, stunt flying not included. Any other exclusions you want, just say the word. Meanwhile, if there's any company details you might like to know, just ask. Jeanie, I've been thinking, watching our otters...'

'Are you sure there were otters?'

'There were otters. Jeanie, I really would like to share. I'm not sure how to yet, but I need to try. If you trust me, that is. If you'd trust me to share, to love you, to hold you in honour...'

'And make me watch invisible otters? And help me fly?'

'Yes. Yes and yes and yes.'

There was another silence then, longer than the last. The whole world seemed to be holding its breath. Alasdair had almost forgotten how to breathe. This slip of a woman, this sprite, his amazing Jeanie, she held his heart in the palm of her hand.

'I don't suppose,' she said, diffidently now, gesturing to the dilapidated cottage behind them, 'that you thought to lay the fire?'

'No,' he said, reluctantly. 'This morning got a bit busy.'

'You so need a partner.' And amazingly her eyes twinkled with laughter and he felt his heart lurch with the beginnings of joy. 'I guess…we could make do without. It's not raining. The pasture up here is nice and soft, and if we wander around the next headland, the curve of the cove makes it private.'

'Are you suggesting what I think you might be suggesting?'

'I might be,' she said demurely. 'Though we'll need to ring Maggie's mam to deal with the guests.'

'I already did,' he said and he smiled at her and she smiled right back. Shared laughter…the best part of loving bar none.

But then she turned and looked towards the faraway castle, high on the headland in the distance, and her face twisted with something he didn't understand.

'Lady of Duncairn Castle,' she said softly, at last. 'I don't think I'll be very good at it.'

'No castle ever had a lady more worthy. Jeanie, I love you.'

'I love you, too,' she said softly. 'Otters or not. Wealth or not. Castle or not. Eileen would be pleased.'

'I'll bet she knows,' he told her and, enough, it was time. A man had to do what a man had to do. He was the Lord of Duncairn and this was his lady. His wife. He swept her up and held her in his arms and stood for a long, long moment on the crag over the burn, looking out over the sea.

And something settled in his heart, something so deep and so pure that he felt almost as if he were being reborn.

'If I was Tarzan right now, I suspect I'd beat my chest and yodel,' he told his love, and she chuckled and looped her arms around his neck and held.

'Don't you dare drop me.'

'I wouldn't,' he told her and he kissed her then, long and deep and hard, with all the love in his heart, with all the tenderness he could summon, with all the joy of the future in the link between them.

And then he turned and carried his lady to the waiting wild grasses of Duncairn Island.

The two eagles soared on the thermals, and two otters drifted lazily downstream again, at one with their world, at peace.

It didn't matter. The world continued apace. The Lord and Lady of Duncairn might know in their hearts that all was well on their estate, but for now they weren't watching. They were otherwise engaged.

And they were otherwise engaged for a very long time.

* * * * *

MILLS & BOON®
Large Print – November 2015

The Ruthless Greek's Return
Sharon Kendrick

Bound by the Billionaire's Baby
Cathy Williams

Married for Amari's Heir
Maisey Yates

A Taste of Sin
Maggie Cox

Sicilian's Shock Proposal
Carol Marinelli

Vows Made in Secret
Louise Fuller

The Sheikh's Wedding Contract
Andie Brock

A Bride for the Italian Boss
Susan Meier

The Millionaire's True Worth
Rebecca Winters

The Earl's Convenient Wife
Marion Lennox

Vettori's Damsel in Distress
Liz Fielding

MILLS & BOON®
Large Print – December 2015

The Greek Demands His Heir
Lynne Graham

The Sinner's Marriage Redemption
Annie West

His Sicilian Cinderella
Carol Marinelli

Captivated by the Greek
Julia James

The Perfect Cazorla Wife
Michelle Smart

Claimed for His Duty
Tara Pammi

The Marakaios Baby
Kate Hewitt

Return of the Italian Tycoon
Jennifer Faye

His Unforgettable Fiancée
Teresa Carpenter

Hired by the Brooding Billionaire
Kandy Shepherd

A Will, a Wish...a Proposal
Jessica Gilmore

1115 Rom LP

MILLS & BOON®

Why shop at millsandboon.co.uk?

Each year, thousands of romance readers find their perfect read at mIllsandboon.co.uk. That's because we're passionate about bringing you the very best romantic fiction. Here are some of the advantages of shopping at www.millsandboon.co.uk:

* **Get new books first**—you'll be able to buy your favourite books one month before they hit the shops

* **Get exclusive discounts**—you'll also be able to buy our specially created monthly collections, with up to 50% off the RRP

* **Find your favourite authors**—latest news, interviews and new releases for all your favourite authors and series on our website, plus ideas for what to try next

* **Join in**—once you've bought your favourite books, don't forget to register with us to rate, review and join in the discussions

Visit **www.millsandboon.co.uk**
for all this and more today!